IDLE CURIOSITY

ALSO BY MARTHA BERGLAND

A Farm under a Lake

Idle Curiosity

by

MARTHA BERGLAND

GRAYWOLF PRESS

Publication of this volume is made possible in part by a grant
provided by the Minnesota State Arts Board through an
appropriation by the Minnesota State Legislature, and by a grant
from the National Endowment for the Arts. Significant additional
support has been provided by the Andrew W. Mellon Foundation,
the Lila Wallace-Reader's Digest Fund, the McKnight Foundation,
and other generous contributions from foundations, corporations,
and individuals. To these organizations and individuals who make
our work possible, we offer heartfelt thanks.

Published by Graywolf Press
2402 University Avenue, Suite 203
Saint Paul, Minnesota 55114
All rights reserved.
www.graywolfpress.org

Published in the United States of America

ISBN 1-55597-257-8

2   4   6   8   9   7   5   3   1
First Graywolf Printing, 1997

Library of Congress Catalog Card Number: 96-78744

Special funding for this title provided by the Jerome Foundation.

Two sections of this novel appeared in slightly different form in
Wisconsin Academy Review, Spring 1993, Volume 39, Number 2.

Cover design: Nora L. Koch

Cover art: Richard Krogstad, "Loess Hills 39-1" oil/paper, 1996

For Larry Barnett
and for Hugh and Elizabeth Bergland

IDLE CURIOSITY

1

In front of the white clapboard hotel that for ninety years housed the transients of Half Moon, Illinois stood a tiny old man in a red-and-white-striped bathrobe, the belt tied tight, his hands knotted together through the pockets. It was Ed Check, gazing at the lazy traffic of sparrows and bugs, box-elder seeds and cottonwood fluff under the old trees on Main Street. His toes—he wore black socks and no shoes—curled and uncurled over the crumbling curb. Stepping down to the brick street, he changed from idle looking to the mildest waiting. Ed Check lived in the hotel with other retired farmers and widowers from Half Moon and the farms around.

The air that morning was sweet with the scent of all the rich land it had drifted across. Ed turned his face southwest into the breeze, smiled into it, wondering what air Marlene breathed this morning and where, and what air his little girl breathed, and his middle girl; the oldest was safe here in town. This air, he knew, had passed not long before over his farm, over what had been his farm.

The breeze riffled through a magazine left open on the floor of the hotel porch and rummaged through Ed's soft, sparse hair. For a moment Ed wished his former wife would drive by and see him in his pajamas and robe on the sidewalk. That would have her huffing and ruffled for a week. Then Ed Check lifted his chin when he remembered again to wait; he took his hands from his pockets and waited harder.

Early this morning he had dreamed of one of his girls—he was too far away to see which one—as she disappeared over the top of a hill. He had made his legs push himself toward her, but the hill itself rose soft and alive in front of him, and each step just sunk his feet deeper.

Ed had woken up in the dark, gasping, his blood making that racket in his ears, so he had kept his eyes closed and slowed down his breaths and began to take himself back out to the farm. From Half Moon out to the farm, he flew through the dark, cutting across all the straight lines below. He breathed slowly to make himself just float again over the square of field where the house used to be, though he knew that really it was summer and he was in his sofa bed at the Half Moon Hotel. He kept his eyes closed so he could stay out there in the air where the house had been. Then he let himself down easy. It was fourteen years ago last March that Marlene had taken Vickie and left, so it was always March when he let himself down onto the field.

It was March in the fields. The ground was thawing, softening, exhaling that cold spring breath. Geese were out in the stubble and the shallow ponds. He made himself hear the low commotion of them out there eating, muttering, poking in the mud. They were stopped on their way north. Then Ed let himself know that Marlene was out there, and Vickie, too. Vickie was still six years old. They were both coming toward him—a small old man in pajamas.

That was when he opened his eyes, when he saw that he was imagining an old man in pajamas in the middle of a field. That was him, Ed Check, now, unbelievably, an old man. And he knew there was no way he could call to his wife and his daughter. They did what they wanted or they did what they could; his wanting them back didn't move them at all. He didn't even know where they were.

When he opened his eyes, he got up and put on his bathrobe and lay down again to watch for the sun to light up the mirror on the west wall.

He had been lying still a long time when there was a soft knock on his door. He didn't say Come in. He wouldn't have to, because it was Marlene coming back as he had been dreaming she would. The woman came in and before she was half in the door he knew it was not Marlene; it was his middle girl, Janet. She sat down next to him quietly, and he sat up and smiled. She was the one in the dream. He put his hand on her hand. He hadn't seen Janet in months. "What's wrong?" he said. "Jannie, what's wrong?" He switched on the lamp by his bed.

"Nothing, really," she said. "I just came to see you."

"In the middle of the night? Where's Jack?"

"In Wisconsin, still at home. I had to drive this lady I've been taking care of down to her daughter's in Quincy yesterday and then I just came over here to see you." He could hear in her voice that this wasn't the whole story. She was more quiet and delicate than usual in her voice and her motions, trying to disturb him and the night as little as possible.

"Let's go outside," he said, "watch the sun come up."

"Fine," she said. "I'll wait in the hall while you get dressed."

"I *am* dressed," Ed said. "Let's go." Janet wore her jeans and a T-shirt, and she carried over her shoulder some kind of purse that looked like it was knitted out of twine.

"You're in your pajamas," she said, and then her voice had in it that liveliness. In the gray light he saw that she was smiling at him, yet her arms were tight at her sides and her hands shoved into her pockets like she was cold, maybe shivering.

"I got my bathrobe on. Edith—your former mother—used to go out in her nightgown. Remember?"

"That was in the country, Dad, and she's still my mother. She's only 'former' for you."

"I suppose," he said as he retied his bathrobe. He could see Edith stooping in a row of lettuces, her cotton nightgown dragging in front on the wet ground, the sun through the thin gown showing her breasts swinging loose. Like squashes. He could feel that this wouldn't be a good day for his hands.

They went out the front of the Half Moon Hotel, and at the top of the steps he paused. There was not a dog on the street or a car. And no smell of cooking yet. No televisions on. Just the damp rising in mists. Quiet and gray and green, the street silver, like the trail of a slug. Janet had gone on ahead of him.

From the back she looked like what she'd always been to Ed—a Check, a child, skinny and wiry and too slight to deal with the world. Ed shivered. But she was a Hawn now, married to Jack, who up to recently always seemed to Ed to stand between Janet and the terrors of the world. And she was a grown woman, for Christ's sake. She could have children, though she didn't have any for reasons he couldn't ask about. He started down the step and stopped. Janet was almost *too old* to have children. He shivered again and pulled his robe tighter around him.

When he caught up to her, they went down the block to the bench by the sidewalk. "Let's sit here at the bus stop," he said. "Take the first one that comes along." He swiped a little at the dew on the green bench before they sat down.

"We might wait awhile," she said, "since there aren't any buses in Half Moon." They fell so easily, Ed thought, into their old way of talking to each other.

"Let's wait anyway," he said. They sat without talking

in a silence as easy as their talk, and watched the sun come up—bright pink and full blown—beyond Half Moon's hills, between St. Rose's steeple and the cupola on the courthouse.

"What day is it?" he asked. The light did not look like a weekday's light.

"Monday," she said.

"Monday? Doesn't feel like Monday." He looked down the street toward St. Rose's, and it seemed like the kind of light the Catholics would like for one of their wedding processions—gold and kind of holy. After they were married, Jack and Janet had walked along that sidewalk to the usual big blowout at the hotel.

"Remember that weird deal about your wedding procession?" Ed asked Janet. "Remember what happened right over there?" He remembered perfectly well. He wanted to ask her what the trouble was, but he couldn't yet.

"Sure, the skirt tore off my dress." There was irritation in her voice, but he couldn't tell who it was aimed at.

"Right. Somebody stepped on your . . . the tail end of your skirt. Right over there, if I remember correctly." Ed pointed across the street.

"Train," she said. "I wore a dress with a damned train." She shook her head. "I must have been somebody else then."

"You were a bride." He took her hand and held it so it warmed both of his. Everybody was somebody else then.

The sun was caught up in the tops of the trees now, in what Ed liked to think of as the trees' tresses. He'd read that somewhere, but it was not something you could say out loud. He saw Marlene's hair fall across her face as she leaned over him. Some might call her hair just a medium brown, but if it was between you and the light, you could see colors there like in the grain of oak.

"What are we waiting for?" he asked after a while.

"We're waiting for Jack," she said.

Ed knew this was Janet telling him why she had come back. A scout she was for the two of them, or a pigeon. But how long, he wondered, did she mean to wait, because Jack was a stubborn man, not likely to come home just because someone asked him to, even if the someone was Janet, his wife. And was Jack still a good idea for Janet? He had been. Ed remembered being sure of that. Twenty years ago, when it looked like Jack had nothing but good luck and good times ahead of him, Jack seemed like the right man for Janet. But a man's luck changes. What kind of thinking is this? Ed asked himself. And he stood up to go back in.

When they went back to the Half Moon, they looked for Bill, who managed the place for Edith, and they got Janet a nice room on the second floor so she could get some sleep. Then Ed went back to his room and surprised himself by going back to sleep and waking up late in the morning. "Like a rich bastard," he said to the mirror where the sun had been hours before.

"A day with two nights," he said as he pulled the bedclothes off his sofa and stuffed them into the closet.

He had tried to get into his clean pants, but they'd starched them again; hell, they were practically laminated. He couldn't pry the layers apart. "Not opposable anymore," he said of his stiff thumbs.

So he had gone out front of the hotel in his robe and pajamas to wait for a hand and to leave behind in his dim room the stale air of sleeping too long. He waited with the sun on his scalp and his face; he squinted and nearly dozed. Everything was loose and unraveling but his hands.

After a while, the racket of a car headed down Main Street, an air-cooled engine from the sound of things, and he was right—a pale blue, rusted-out Volkswagen Beetle Ed had never seen before. The VW passed Ed on the other side of the street, then slowed, made a snappy, one-armed U-turn, pulled up right next to Ed, and stopped. When the driver ducked his head low to see out the passenger-side window, Ed took his hands out of his pockets. He took a deep breath. This wasn't who, but what, he'd been waiting for: Anyone would do.

The driver rolled down the window and asked, "Can you tell me how to get to Dr. John Fowler's office?"

Ed leaned down and looked in the car. "Beg pardon," he said.

The man in the car continued. "The office of the optometrist, John Fowler. All I have is the name of a building and the name of the town. Flaherty Building. Half Moon." The man was young, Ed saw, not past forty, maybe closer to thirty. In the same hand that held the steering wheel, the man had a piece of paper with the information on it. The other hand held his glasses and he rubbed his eyes with the heel of that hand.

Ed rested his hands on the car door. "John Fowler? His office?" Ed knew he had never seen this man before. "Why don't you try the new eye doctor?" he asked. "A woman, it is. She works out of the strip mall outside of town." The news of the death of Fowler—if it was not good news—could not possibly be of more than minor interest to anyone.

Under the cover of some talk about the new woman optometrist, Ed allowed his gaze to roam over this stranger and the contents of his car. The man was from out of state—his license plates told Ed that—but he hadn't gotten a chance to see which state. "A cosmopolitan fellow like yourself from . . . ?"

"Massachusetts."

". . . from Massachusetts wouldn't mind going to a woman, but a lot of these old guys from the country have trouble with that." Ed was exaggerating his Midwestern twang; he thought this man might expect it, appreciate it. The stranger put his glasses on, then took them off again and with one finger carefully rubbed the inside corner of one eye, then the other. Ed saw that the man's eyes were red like they had done all his work, and, still talking about the woman optometrist, he noticed in the man's backseat some heavy books whose titles he couldn't see, reference books or law books or something; cassette tapes—one was Patsy Cline; a wadded-up jacket, and a Celtics cap. And there were soda cans and papers and Styrofoam cartons—all the trash that accumulates in a car when you drive for a few days. It smelled like mustard and coffee.

"So that didn't happen to you?" Ed asked him.

"What?" The man leaned toward Ed, wrapping his right arm around the back of the passenger seat.

"You didn't get something in your eye? That's not why you're going to the optometrist?"

"No." The man smiled.

Ed saw that though the man was tired, his eyes were friendly behind those funny old-fashioned spectacles, and there were gold lights in his light brown eyes, like foil was behind them. Marlene had that metallic color in her eyes, too, but with her it was more green.

Then there was that feeling that meant he was just about to remember something. For a breathless moment this almost-knowing swung around dangerous and loose inside of him. He thought the man might have to do with Marlene coming back or with finding Vickie, but he settled down when he realized the man had to do with Edith. He knew who this man was; this was Edith's optometrist, her new tenant. She had been writing to him and talking to him on the phone for months about the office, about taking over Fowler's practice. But Ed had to make sure.

Looking down at the brick street between the car and

the curb, he took a deep breath and then, squinting, carefully watched the man's face. "You know," Ed said, "John Fowler's dead. Dead not too long ago, but dead just the same." What he saw on the man's face was a grimace, but no surprise.

"I know . . ."

Ed didn't let him finish. "I know who you are." Ed stood up straight. "You're the new optometrist. You're Alvin somebody."

The man opened the car door and, unfolding himself, got out of the car and stood up.

The man was very tall. Ed stood and just looked. How could a guy that big get in that car in the first place? The man reached right across the hood of the Volkswagen and shook Ed's hand. "I'm Nelson Alvin," he said. "Rhymes with ball peen."

"Ed Check, just the way it sounds," said Ed, staring and backing away toward the hotel behind him. A fisherman feels like this when he catches a fish twice as big as he expects. "Come on in here a minute," Ed said. He felt his knees wobble in his baggy pajamas. "I'll get dressed and take you to where you want to go. I was waiting for somebody to help me with something anyway."

While Nelson Alvin pulled out of the loading zone and parked his car, Ed continued in a louder voice, his hands again in his bathrobe pockets, while he backed slowly up the brick walk. "Janet's still asleep," he said. "She's my daughter; she just got in late last night from up north, Wisconsin. And I'm not about to ask one of those old bastards in there." He pointed with his head back at the hotel behind him.

This man Nelson Alvin was not in a hurry. When he got out of the car this time, he stretched his arms above and then behind him, groaning with pleasure and cracking some knuckles and joints. Then he shut the car door and leaned for a moment on the roof and looked. Nelson Alvin's smile, his mildness and the mass of him, the real interest he seemed to take—all stopped time for Ed, made him see this place as if for the first time.

Though he was facing Nelson and the street, Ed could see through Nelson's eyes the graceful porch of the big old hotel, its long, elegant windows trimmed in green, and the pillars that you could almost call columns. He saw the big evergreens at either side of the hotel framing and cooling it. He saw the graceful silver maples, and then he saw the air itself, saw it as a hot, thick suspension through which silver maple seeds spun slowly like tatters of green light. All the stuff in all the dense air— the fluff and bugs and chaff from elm flowers—floated as if in suspension. He floated too—in front of a hotel in the Midwest in the middle of a day in June, fumbling with the knot on his bathrobe.

Then Nelson Alvin came around the car and leaned on the hood. Ed couldn't contain himself. "My God," he said, "you are tall!" He couldn't take his eyes off Nelson. He walked backward a bit up the sidewalk. The grass was long between the bricks, and the anthills were warm under his feet.

A green-winged seed stuck in Nelson's hair and Nelson brushed it away. Under the huge trees and before the shaggy hotel, Nelson was, of the two of them, the one in scale.

"You're about the tallest man I've ever seen." Ed, standing on the middle step, was eye-to-eye with Nelson.

"I'm not that tall," said Nelson.

"Well, maybe not, but you're pretty tall," Ed said. "How tall are you?"

"About five feet seventeen," Nelson said, grinning.

"Six foot five."

"Right."

Face-to-face with the man, Ed let himself stare. Nelson had pale skin like a girl, clean brown hair, fans of wrinkles in the thin skin around his eyes. Ed looked in his face for the sharp edges or shadows, the little jerking muscles or blinks that cover evasion or lies or worse, but he saw none of that. He saw a man not at all self-conscious, a stranger who was right at home, a sweet person you could put to your own uses and he wouldn't even mind. It made Ed wonder and he stepped back. A blue jay fussed in a cedar tree by the porch. Ed opened the screen door. "I'm in here," he said.

Nelson followed Ed into the lobby of the Half Moon Hotel, which, though the doors and long windows were open, smelled of turpentine and old cigar smoke. From about a third of the old walnut paneling, layers of green paint had been stripped, and scaffolding was in place, Ed explained, to take out the 1950s lowered ceiling. "It will be a nice room one of these years." They turned out of the lobby into a shiny yellow, fluorescent-lit hallway. Here the doors and woodwork were darkened with decades of varnish. Ed's sock feet and Nelson's basketball shoes were silent on the linoleum tile. As they passed closed and partially closed doors, Ed heard the air conditioners and fans, televisions low or loud, the farm report. It was noon.

The door to Number 6, Ed's room, was ajar. It was a corner room with windows on two sides, but dark because the light from the east was cut off by the porch, and from the south by the cedar trees where the jay still fussed.

Ed motioned Nelson to have a seat on the sofa in front of them, between two piles of neatly folded, professionally laundered clothes. But Nelson stood looking at Ed's framed aerial photo of the farm, while Ed padded over to a big easy chair and picked up the pair of green work pants laying stiff-legged across the arms. "Heavy starch," said Ed, and Nelson turned and smiled. "That picture"— Ed nodded at it—"that's where we used to live, back to my grandparents."

"You farmed?" Nelson asked.

"That's right," Ed said. "All my life until I stopped." The farm was like a part of his body that he never let show; it felt like something embarrassing he had kept that everyone thought he had got rid of. He held the pants up by one corner. "It's the goddamned zipper. I can't get it open or unstuck. Arthritis."

He handed the sheet of pants to Nelson, who stood and held them against himself and fumbled with the zipper. Ed thought they looked like doll pants in front of Nelson.

Nelson freed the zipper and handed the pants to Ed, who climbed down into them as you would step into parallel postholes. Then he took off his bathrobe and hung it on a book that was pulled partway out of a bookshelf for that purpose. Ed noticed in the mirror that his bare chest was so white that he looked like one of those blind fish in caves, and he said so to Nelson.

Nelson stood there like he helped old men in small towns everyday unstick their zippers. He looked ready for whatever might happen next, but he didn't seem very curious about it.

While Ed buttoned his shirt, he told Nelson about his room. "It isn't big, but I've got everything I need. It doesn't look like it, but I've got four rooms here, no, five. I'll show you. This wall here, the north wall, as you can see, is my kitchen." And, to demonstrate, Ed turned on the faucet in the little sink and opened the door to the small refrigerator under it. "This here is the bathroom," and he opened the bathroom door. "Help yourself, by the way, if you need to." Then Ed took a pair of shoes off the little kitchen table, pulled out a rickety blue chair and sat down there to put his shoes on. "The south wall, where you are . . . ," Ed was a little out of breath, ". . . is the living room. And the east wall . . . ," he nodded toward the wall that was just off the hotel porch, "is my attic or closet. All them boxes you see are my stuff." Ed stood up, bending his knees a few times to force them into the starched creases. "The west wall over there is my library." He buttoned the cuffs of his starched white shirt. "I'd like to be able to tell you that all those are my books, but they are my daughter's and her husband's. I've had them books since they got out of college more than twenty years ago. There's about everything you'd want to know, I guess, about agriculture in the 1960s and French poems and some other things like psychology and sociology—the good parts all marked up in yellow to save you wear and tear. Every time they move to a new place they tell me this time they'll come get their books, but I stopped believing them about ten years ago, and now I don't think I'd even let them have them. Books add a little class to the place and, besides, I take one out now and again and read it."

Ed was dressed. "Be right out," Ed said and he went in the bathroom and shut the door.

He stood a moment leaning on the sink. Though he was dimly reflected in the mirror—Ed had never gotten in the habit of turning a light on when he entered a room—he didn't see himself; he saw that Janet coming home and this new optometrist coming had changed everything, probably for the better. So why did he feel so tired and want to just lean on the sink in the dark? He sighed and washed his face and wetted his hair and slicked it back.

When he came out of the bathroom with his hair wet and harrowed, and his white shirt damp in spots and pink where it stuck to his skin, the optometrist was standing by the bookshelf with his hands behind his back, looking at Ed's row of framed pictures on a shelf. Ed went over and stood beside him and then gently pushed him back to the beginning of the row. "This first one here is my oldest girl, Mary. Red-haired like her mom. Mary lives a few blocks over that way in a little house next to the Catholic church. She's my church girl. She's been divorced so long, people think she's an old maid, and maybe she thinks so too. She's a good girl, but she doesn't know how to have fun." He pointed Nelson to the next one. "This is my middle girl, Janet, and her husband, Jack, on their wedding day. The reception was right here in this hotel. They live up in Wisconsin, but now Jannie is upstairs asleep, home for a visit."

Ed paused. Nelson stood in front of a photograph of a thick young woman and a little girl standing in tall grass. They both squinted in bright sun. "These?" Nelson asked.

"That is Marlene, my second wife, and our girl, Vickie. That was taken about fifteen years ago."

"Do they live here?" Nelson asked.

"They're in the South," Ed told him. Then he steered him toward the door. "So you're the new optometrist. Not a minute too soon, I'll have to tell you. Any longer and we'd all be in the habit of going to the eye doctor in the mall, but a young go-getter like you will be able to handle the competition. And she is, so far, your only competition." Ed put his wallet in his hip pocket. "Come on, son, let's get you started."

Directing Nelson to the door with a slight bow and a formal openhanded gesture, Ed felt a little like one of those cast-iron grooms, and Nelson bowed back. "You must have a million questions and here I've been doing all the talking. I'll show you first where your office is and introduce you to your landlady, Edith Flaherty, God help you, and then I'll buy you some lunch."

Outside, they stopped on the hotel porch and stood for a moment. Ed felt a diagonal line drawn from the top of his head to the top of Nelson's head. They must look funny together; they sure took up an odd-shaped space.

When they left the hotel, headed for the Flaherty Building up on the square, Ed pointed out some of the big frame houses built in the 1870s—one now a funeral parlor, another a lawyer's home and office, another boarded up and for sale. "Railroad money built them," he told Nelson. "Here's the old station," and he steered Nelson over to a parapet on the side of the hill, where they stood a moment and looked down through the box-elder scrub and sumac to the tracks below. "One train a day," Ed said. "Used to be six."

"This is really a pretty town," said Nelson, turning around and looking up and down the street. "As pretty as those New England villages, but I like it better. It's not so fixed up and fake somehow."

"No, you couldn't call Half Moon fixed up or fake," Ed said, looking at the pickup trucks parked in front of the old Beale house. Erie Beale's grandfather, the judge, had built that big house, but now Chuckie Kanfer had a machine shop out in back and Jewel Kanfer ran a junk shop out of the front.

Though Ed panted on the hill, soon they were in the square looking up at the courthouse steeple and at the fancy water fountains, while Ed explained to Nelson that Edith Flaherty, who owned the Flaherty Building, also owned the Half Moon Hotel and who knows what else in Half Moon. He also said that dealing with Edith would take a certain alertness on Nelson's part and that he, Ed, ought to know as she was his former wife.

Ed and Nelson came into Edith's dark little offices on the ground floor of the Flaherty Building, blinking after the bright light of the square. With his hand on Nelson's elbow, Ed steered Nelson to the front of the secretary's desk. "Deb Whiteside," Ed said to the blond woman behind the desk, "this is Dr. Nelson Alvin. Optometrist. He'll be upstairs in Fowler's old office. He'll have to talk to her," and he nodded toward the closed door.

Nelson reached forward and shook Deb's hand, which startled her out of her seat, and then all three of them stood a moment and listened to the voice coming through the closed door. They could hear, not the words, but the tone of a woman's hearty voice—wheedling and cajoling, rising in anger and threatening, lowering, consoling, and then, Ed knew, insincerely apologizing.

"Poor bastard," Ed muttered, and Deb giggled.

Ed turned to Nelson. "We'll just have to cool our heels a bit until she finishes off whoever it is. Have a seat, Nelson." But Nelson went behind one of the chairs and stood looking out the window at the square.

Deb and Ed looked at Nelson's broad back for a moment and then Deb, raising her eyebrows, nodded her silent approval and interest to Ed. Ed realized how attractive Nelson would be to women—his strong back and arms, his clean brown hair, those sad eyes, and the way he seemed to almost apologize for his size.

Ed sighed and sat down on the corner of Deb's desk. "So, Deb, what's going on with that kid of yours? You need me to come over and whale the daylights out of Dale?"

Deb slumped at her desk. "Oh, Ed, now he's twice as big as you or me. All you could do is what I do—bail him out of jail now and then on Sunday mornings."

"I guess it'll take somebody bigger than either of us," and Ed nodded toward Nelson.

Then Deb pointed at the ring finger of her left hand and mouthed the question, "Married?"

Ed shrugged, embarrassed. He hadn't noticed or asked or even thought to ask Nelson Alvin if he was married. The idea of his powers slipping like that depressed him. "I can't quite figure what drives these kids to drink," he said. "Doesn't seem like they've lived long enough to have to. How's Carl?" he asked Deb and then wished he hadn't. The subject of drinking was what reminded him of Carl, and he wasn't sure anyway if he was supposed to know that Deb Whiteside and Carl were going out now and then.

"Carl's my son-in-law," he said across the room to Nelson in case Deb didn't want to answer.

"No, he's not, Ed," Deb said.

"He is, too. Carl is my son-in-law."

"How come? He's not married to any of your daughters."

"He's the brother of the man married to one of my daughters. If Jack is my son-in-law and Carl is the brother of my son-in-law, then that makes him, to my mind, my son-in-law." While he talked, Ed watched Deb smile at Nelson in a bright, cockeyed way she'd never smiled at him. Deb meant business.

At that moment the door to the office opened, and Edith Flaherty stood beside it looking behind her; out came a reluctant, red-faced farmer, seed-corn cap in hand. He hadn't said a word that anyone could hear. All were silent until the farmer slammed the office door behind him, setting its frosted glass rattling.

Edith stood beside her door a moment longer than was necessary, a frieze on a big vase—one arm cocked on her hip, her face rusty red, her brown knit dress a little too tight, her orange scarf bright and her red hair bright.

"Edith!" Ed said, hopping off the desk. "You look positively combustible today!"

She ignored Ed. She hadn't seen Nelson. "Deb, get out Jim Massey's lease, the latest one." Then she nodded at Ed and, on her way back into her office, said, "OK, Ed, come on in for a minute."

Ed flushed and didn't move. He called after her. "I've brought somebody here to see you. Dr. Nelson Alvin has arrived this morning from Massachusetts."

Edith turned and gave Ed a dark look that made him smile, though he knew it was a small victory—being the first to meet the new optometrist.

Then without looking at him, she walked in front of Ed, who took in again her scent and the little abrasive sounds of her stockings. As she walked toward Nelson— she couldn't see his face; he stood against the light—her posture, her body, seemed to soften, her ferocity seemed to melt, and the woman who strode toward Nelson was warm and generous. Ed leaned against the doorway.

"Dr. Alvin," Edith said, pronouncing it wrong. "Welcome to Half Moon!" And she took his hand in both of hers.

Deb and Ed looked at each other while Edith pulled Nelson past them into her office. Ed hated his pleading tone, but he said, "Make your business quick because Nelson and I are going to lunch in a few minutes."

"Oh, Ed, it's too late for that. We've got too much to talk about, Dr. Alvin and I." She called this back to Ed from the office. Then she put her head out the door and said to Deb, "Go over to the café and get us a couple of sandwiches, will you, dear?"

Nelson was standing in Edith's office framed in the doorway. "Ed," he said. "I'll pick you up for dinner tonight. You can show me the nightlife."

Edith came around her desk. "You will do no such thing. You will come to dinner at my place. There's people you ought to meet. We'll get you off on the right foot and fill you in on who's who and what's what around here."

Ed strode right into Edith's office and Edith backed off behind her desk. He spoke to Nelson with his back to Edith. "Don't worry about it," he said. "You'd better go with her. Getting off on her right foot takes some doing and there's no way to do it but her way. We'll have plenty of time later. I'll go out to dinner tonight," and here his voice raised, "with my daughter, who got in town this morning at four o'clock."

Edith came around from behind the desk and took Ed's hand. Her eyebrows were ornate with worry. "Janet?" she asked. "Is she OK? What is she doing here? Is Jack with her? Why didn't she call me?"

Ed was smiling a smile that wasn't going to tell Edith a thing. She dropped his hand and took a step back and now her face was brick red. "Maybe you didn't mean my daughter, Janet, but that woman Marlene's girl. Vickie. Is she here, Ed? If so, how did you recognize her? It's been quite a while since you've seen her, hasn't it?"

"I hear from her; she's in Florida," Ed said quietly, then he just shook his head, denying, not what she said, but her tone, her talking like this in front of anyone. "Edith," he said. "Edith."

A moment passed. "Janet's here?" she asked quietly, the venomous tone gone.

"Yes."

"Is she all right?"

"I think so."

"Ed," Edith said, trying to start over, "Why don't you come to dinner tonight, too, you and Janet. You should be there and you haven't seen my new house since it's been finished and I moved in. I'd like it if you came. All right, Ed?"

Ed waited a moment. "OK, Edith. What time?"

"Is six OK?"

"Six is fine. Janet and I will be there at six." He turned to Nelson. "Where are you going to stay?"

Edith and Ed looked at each other. "I thought the hotel," she said.

"That would be good," Ed said.

"The suite?" she asked Ed.

"The suite would be very good. Get him back to the hotel in time to unload his car and rest a little. The man's tired from driving."

When Ed left Edith's office he walked across the courthouse square, past the Civil War cannon, the World War I statue, and the World War II plaque. Two young mothers in shorts, women Ed didn't know, languidly pushed their babies in strollers to the donut shop. Old Mrs. Parrot stepped smartly across the brick street. Francis and James O'Connor—both wearing white short-sleeved shirts and brown pants—came out of the insurance office and waved to Ed as they crossed the square. There were more people than cars in the square.

Just before he went into the café, Ed turned and looked back at the Flaherty Building, but he couldn't see anything through the windows. The Flaherty Building was both bald-faced and ornate—big, plain, double-hung windows and a broad red-brick facade. Set over each of the plain windows was a fancy Victorian lintel. And the third floor was under a gray mansard roof. Then Ed laughed out loud. Edith looked just like her building: tall, with wide red planes in her face and that rust-colored knit dress; elaborate eyebrows set over dark unreadable eyes; and he knew that underneath the red dye was wiry slate-colored hair.

Ed went into the café grinning, hoping there would be somebody there to tell that to, but the lunch crowd was gone, the café was empty except for the waitress, and she turned out to be new and someone Ed didn't know. She was from Indiana, Ed found out, and had come here with her husband, who managed the shoe department in the BuyMor outside of town.

2

Vickie could smell the last couple of days on him—the greasy plastics factory where he worked, the sweat he'd sweated, beers he'd drunk and pissed, cigarettes he'd smoked. He was in front of her like the trunk of a tree. At either side of his shoulders the bare room and the Gulf air and the new walls seemed bland to Vickie, seemed to have inhaled a breath and held it, seemed to wait, and, worst of all, seemed to have turned away. She had seen so goddamned many people whose faces bore the expression that the room seemed to hold. She was so tired of it all. As she sagged against the wall, it seemed as if she'd always been right here, and Bo had always been right there in front of her like a big tree, and for all she cared she could wait until some time in the next century when he would be struck by lightning. For a moment she had a very clear picture of a tree on Papa Check's farm that had grown around a barbed-wire fence; the wire passed through the wood; the wood engulfed the wire. She didn't know what kind of tree it was, but it wasn't one of these spooky live oaks.

She looked at the room on either side of him, but not at him, not at his face: the inside of his mouth would be bright shiny red, almost like the embarrassing orange around some of those gulls' beaks. She looked now and then at his breast pocket. The design on the pocket—

some kind of tropical fruits printed on turquoise—didn't
match up with the design on his shirt. It was a cheap
shirt, which was a small satisfaction until she remembered it was one she'd bought him. He held her shoulders pinned against the wall, pressed his weight on his
two big hands. He was screaming something at her but
she didn't really hear, not the words; she felt them on her
face, felt his words rough and sharp, scraping at her face.

Beyond him through the sliding door she could see a
pelican veer slowly across the blank square of sky, and
she wondered again why pelicans didn't give everyone
the creeps. They look like pterodactyls, for heaven's
sake; didn't anyone see that but her? The whole place
was scary and cheap. This building had a pool, but every
place in Florida had a pool. Here the balconies fell off
now and then. One woman had broken her back, Vickie
had heard when they first moved in. This woman had
stepped out on her third-floor balcony and it fell off with
her on it. She was paralyzed, they'd said. Vickie wondered for a moment what that woman's life was like, but
that took too much effort and made her realize how
much effort it was taking not to hear him.

And she realized, too, that she was sliding down the
wall, that her feet were in an awkward position, not really supporting her because the groceries she had just
put down on the floor when she had come in were behind her heels, between her heels and the wall. She was
held up by Bo's hands pressing her shoulders against
the wall, by his words hitting her face like grit. He had
never hit her. She just had to wait until it was over. She
could wait, but how long? She thought about trying
to move her feet back so they would be under her, but
even the smallest motion was stopped by a solid bag of
groceries at her heel. What was in that bag? she wondered. There were two bags here, two more were down

in the car, and the car was at the back door of the building with the trunk open and the flashers on. The keys were in one hand, warm and oily, and her purse strap was wrapped tight around the other. The frozen French fries were in the bag at her left heel, along with the ice cream and a gallon of milk and his beer. She tried to get her heel between the two bags so she could get her legs beneath her and stand up straighter, but when she couldn't she laughed at herself. Here you are: The big asshole you live with is throwing the biggest fit ever, your life is completely out of control, and you are trying to make yourself more *comfortable!* The laugh showed on her face and he hit her.

She didn't feel his fist hit her face, but the light in the room flashed and she heard the back of her head hit the wall. She could hear him screaming now, about how it was his, too, and he didn't want it, and what were they going to do with a kid? Thousands of women a day get rid of pregnancies, and what did she think that was in her now, anyway? She heard it, but she had heard it before. He had hit her this time and he had never hit her before; if he hit her once, he would do it again. She didn't think, she just made her face take on the expression of the air and the room. Bland and quiet. And she said in a voice that surprised her, "Honey, you put the beer and ice cream away. I'll get the other stuff out of the car."

He released her. "I'm sorry," he said. "Vickie, I'm sorry."

"I know," she said from the doorway. "But remember that now my name is Lisa."

It wasn't until the beer was put away and he was halfway through the second one that Bo realized that she and his car and the groceries were gone. Later, when he was sober, he would write it off to experience: She was knocked up and the Toyota needed a valve job anyway.

3

Back in his room later that afternoon, Ed had turned on the television and was watching the five o'clock news when Janet came in and sat down beside him on the sofa, leaned her head back, and closed her eyes. It took Janet a long time to wake up; that was the only way she was like her mother. She was small and dark haired like all the Checks, and unlike Edith and all the Flahertys, she would not barge into a room or a life flinging out feelings and opinions and advice. Her face was rosy from sleep, but her skin seemed thinner; he could see new lines beside her eyes and a new tiredness under them. She was not as pretty anymore. There was some liveliness missing. Her hair was too short. He thought of all the farm women he had known in the old days who just hacked off their hair because they thought nice hair wasn't worth the trouble anymore.

The commercials came on and Ed hit the mute button on his remote control and touched Janet's shoulder. She opened her eyes and turned her head toward him. "Listen, Jan, did you hear the one about the two cannibals eating lunch?" She smiled and shook her head. "Two cannibals eating lunch and one turns to the other and says, 'How's your mother-in-law?' 'Not too good,' he says. 'Well,' says the first one, 'then just eat the noodles.'"

Janet laughed a little laugh that was more like a cough.

The commercials were over. Ed put the volume up again. It was some feature about a little boy with leukemia. The people in the town where he lived had got money together to send him to Disney World. Ed said, "Janet, don't you wish that dying children or their parents could come up with something else besides Disney World to wish for?"

He glanced again at Janet and saw that her eyes were closed again. He no longer knew the details of what caused her to feel the way she did, but he still could tell at a glance what it was she felt. Ed knew few facts about his daughters' lives, but his connection with them was not through facts. He had seen somewhere pictures of Indian pueblos—houses—carved under and sheltered by the overhang of cliffs. That's where his love for his daughters resided—under the overhang of his ribs. He had the notion that men carried their children in the same place as women, though a little higher under their ribs.

In the old days before Marlene, he had carried all of them—Mary and Janet, and Carl and Jack, who were like his own sons, and even Carl's Surly Shirley and those dopey little kids of theirs. When they all lived out there on the farm around the time Jack and Janet were married, he kept them all safe. He looked out for them all, Mary in her little house in town, and Edith with her one loser boyfriend after another. He couldn't do much more than *look* out for them, but looking had seemed enough until one winter night about twenty years ago.

It was an evening when Jack and Janet had asked everybody out for supper—Carl and Shirley and the kids, Mary, and even Edith was there—because of some boyfriend, she was too miserable to sit alone at home, even though Marlene was there too. So the house was full of noise and action, most of it in the kitchen. It was one of those bitter cold evenings when everything out under the sky was gray and iron hard, so bitter cold that people got boisterous and silly in their houses as one of their ways to fend off the power of the cold. Ed was edgy and the noise of the kids made him nervous, which it didn't usually do. He figured it was just the strain of having Edith and Marlene in the same room. Jack was even more bossy than usual. Usually Ed approved of Jack's bossiness; it meant things would get done, things were underway. But this evening Jack had been critical of Janet leaving the salt out of the potatoes and that had caused some awkwardness at the table, and then Jack was making a big deal out of helping with the dishes when it was clear to Ed that the women just wanted to be in the kitchen by themselves. But Jack wasn't really doing the dishes; he was organizing everybody else to do the dishes. He had a system, some rational way of doing things that didn't let them stack the dishes. He didn't want the clean bottom of a plate to touch the dirty top of another one. So there was Jack in the kitchen or between it and the dining room, in the doorway, in the way. There was his booming voice and his big gestures that people had to duck, and the heat in the house and then a kid or two started crying. Very quickly Shirley took the crying kid upstairs, and Marlene took another kid, and Mary followed.

In the silence left behind, Edith washed plates, splashing a little, while Ed stood in the doorway. Across the room, Jack sat in a kitchen chair, Carl's quiet little boy riding his leg whispering, "Horsey, horsey."

The absence of commotion uncovered a silence that had been eddying around the house all evening. Janet and Carl stood drying dishes, the cloths squeaking on the plates. The silence was between Janet and Carl. The stillness between them enclosed something.

Ed saw it and he was sure of what he saw, and then he saw that Jack saw it too.

Jack stood. He grabbed up Carl's boy. He began swinging him back and forth in the air in front of him—the boy screaming in delight and fear. "Windshield wiper! See, Dad! I'm a windshield wiper!"—back and forth, back and forth, to block out the sight of the two of them, Ed knew, to keep back the waves of knowing. Back and forth and back and forth. Until finally the boy grew pale and clawed at Jack's hands and kicked. Jack let him down in the silence of the room and the boy ran over to his father, clinging to his knees. Carl stood drying a plate. Round and round he wiped the plate and the two brothers just looked at each other, keeping, Ed saw, the knowledge out of their eyes, though it was there in their parallel grim mouths.

Before it could rise to their eyes and they would speak, Ed stepped into the kitchen and pushed past Jack, turning him toward the stove and the window above it. "Jackie," he said, "what're we going to do about this cracked windowpane, boy?" he held Jack tight by the arm. "Jack," Ed had said. "Where's your duct tape?"

That, Ed figured, was the last time he had been able to keep anyone safe. But safe from what, he could now ask, after all these years.

This girl doesn't need this trouble, whatever trouble with Jack brings her here, he said to himself, and reached over and squeezed Janet's shoulder. He realized that for a long time he had assumed that Janet's marriage to Jack was like his marriage to Edith had been. Both Jack and Edith were powerful and childish people whose constant criticisms and small attacks and big defenses kept things moving and in a continual turmoil. So why do we let this go on? Is it cowardice? Pride? Or some virtue? Was what connected them strength or weakness?

It was appalling to Ed that in spite of it all, at that moment as he watched the tired face of his middle girl, the person he envied most in the world was Carl Hawn. Carl lived alone out there in that big empty farmhouse, with almost no furniture, his wife and children gone years ago, he and the cats having almost equal status in the empty rooms. What he envied Carl was the silence and the solitude and the days without public battles; he envied Carl because he was the one of all of them who was able to stay on the farm; he envied Carl for publicly giving up. Was Janet's coming here a way of giving up? Ed was ashamed for hoping so; though Jack was a pain in the neck, he seemed like the son Ed never had, the first son. No, he couldn't wish that his son's wife would leave him. Even for Janet he couldn't wish their marriage ended. And it connected so much besides Jack and Janet.

The news was over. Ed turned off the sound. Janet opened her eyes and smiled at him. "Feel better?" he asked her. She nodded. "Catch up on your sleep?" She nodded again. Then he took a deep breath and said, "I hate to break it to you, but we've going to your mother's for supper."

She looked at him. "Tonight?"

"Tonight. Pretty soon."

"Oh," she said and for a moment she looked out the window beyond Ed. "You got any beer, Dad?"

"You bet." And Ed got up and took two beers out of the little refrigerator below the counter. He opened them, twisting the tops with the towel that covered the arm of the sofa, and handed one to Janet.

"I was at Carl's last night," she said, sitting up to drink her beer.

"When was that?"

"Late. Or early. I drove straight to the farm from this lady, Ina's, in Quincy." Ed waited for her to explain. She was looking out the window beyond him, drinking her beer. "I just had to go see what was left out there, if there was enough left for more of us to make a life from—enough land, I mean, for Jack and me." She looked at Ed. "I wanted to see what was left of Carl. Jack has so little that's good to say about him. I wanted to talk to Carl to see if we could come back. Jack has to have work to do. Four layoffs in six years and now he doesn't even get interviews anymore. He's had so many kinds of jobs now that he doesn't even know what to call himself—an unemployed what? Chemical engineer? Personnel guy? Salesman? And lately, carpenter, roofer, and yard man." Janet got up and went to the hand-colored picture of their farm from the air. "It's hard to think that none of that exists anymore, that the house and outbuildings are gone and it's owned by god-knows-who, that this is a cornfield now."

Ed got up and went to stand beside her. "You always wanted to just live there, didn't you? You and Jack?" She nodded.

"I didn't talk to Carl," she said, moving away from him to lean on the windowsill. "I just walked into the house without knocking and looked around." There were long pauses between her sentences. "He doesn't know I was there. I didn't turn on a light. There were cats all over the place and it seemed sad." Janet looked down at the floor. "I just sat in the living room and thought about things."

Ed didn't mention that he knew Carl slept in the living room.

After a moment she looked up at Ed and smiled and continued. "Then I did what may be a dumb thing. I went into the pantry where the phone is and I shut the door and called Jack. I sat there on the pantry floor just like I was a teenager calling my boyfriend, and I called him. It wasn't dumb to call him, but maybe it was dumb to ask him to come back here, to ask him—without any figures and without talking to Carl—to come back here and try to farm again, the Hawn place."

"You can't think of that, Jannie. It's gone. There's only eighty acres left. And farming is such a heartache, even worse now than when I was farming. You can't make a dime. Jack can't come back to eighty acres."

"I know," she said. "I never was practical about money."

"Carl *lost* most of the land, you know."

"Part of that was our land, Dad."

"It became Carl's land when your mother sold it to him. You and me, honey, were just tenant farmers. Your mom and her aunts were the landlord."

"You know, Dad, Jack has never understood why you and I aren't mad at Carl for screwing up and losing that land back to the bank. He's still mad at Carl for that, for 'becoming a drunk' and losing the Check land and the Hawn land, most of it. But we aren't mad at Carl, are we?" She smiled at him.

"No," Ed said, wondering, "we're not."

"Why is that? Do you know?"

Ed looked at her, surprised that she would ask that question.

"No," he said, "Unless it's just that we love Carl." Then Ed saw in her eyes the question that neither of them asked: Love Carl more than Jack?

They sat for a few minutes. Then Ed said, "Your mom's new house is finished, you know. She moved into it last week."

"Is it nice?"

"I guess so. I've heard it is. I haven't been in it yet, myself."

"You mean she didn't consult you about all the details?" Janet asked. Ed snorted.

They sat for a few minutes watching the silent commercials. "Janet," Ed said, sitting up straighter on the couch. "You can't wear blue jeans to your mother's, not if she's cooking dinner herself. You know how she'll take it."

"Oh, God!"

"Well, you know I'm right."

"I know. I know." Janet put down her beer and got up to go change.

"We taking a fellow with us. I'll go up and get him while you put on a dress." Ed followed Janet out into the hall. "This is that new optometrist Edith has been negotiating for. He's actually a pretty nice guy. Got in town this noon."

"What's his name?" Janet asked.

"Nelson Alvin. 'Rhymes with ball peen.'"

Janet turned and smiled at Ed, the first real smile he'd seen since she got here. "He told you that? 'Rhymes with ball peen'?"

Ed nodded.

"Sounds like a funny guy," Janet said.

"Tall fellow, too," said Ed.

Later, when Janet came back to Ed's room wearing a pale pink dress, Nelson was there. He stood up and shook her hand in the same formal and old-fashioned way that had startled Deb. Ed watched Janet smile at him and relax and try not to show how amazed she was at Nelson's height. He saw that Janet liked him right away, the same way he had. Or they didn't have any reason to dislike him, which may amount to the same thing. "You're too trusting," Edith used to say. "You never give people a chance to prove they're worth anything, Ed, before you tell them your whole life story." "Not enough time," he'd always say. He would tell this guy Nelson just about anything and probably ask him just about anything, and it was the same with Janet. Already Nelson was telling her about his recent divorce, about how he had to get out of the city, and wanted to come back to a small Illinois town. It turned out he had grown up in towns not too far from here, some down near Springfield.

"Let's go, kids," Ed said. "Edith will be burning dinner."

4

Vickie drove north on the interstate until she could calm down and think, until the gas gauge on the Toyota said nearly empty, until the sky on her left was purple and orange and red, and the traffic on the road had begun to thin out. People were eating supper. She pulled off the road and filled the tank and bought some soda and a box of crackers, putting it all on Bo's credit card. This would last only a few days, until he got it together to call up and report the card lost or stolen. When she got back in the car and opened the box of crackers and drank the soda, she realized she had a plan. She was going home to her father. She and this baby would go back to Illinois and maybe the weight of all three of them there—her mother's second and only good husband, her daughter, and her grandchild—would be enough to draw Marlene back where she belonged.

Vickie knew what to do next. She would drive until she found a Burger King near a motel that would take this credit card. She would work as many shifts at Burger King for as many days as she could stand it to get some cash, but she knew the smell of the grease would be hard to take. And the burns from the fryer. And the asshole manager. You had to be an asshole to get to be manager. She wouldn't talk to anyone. She would save up all talk for her father and her baby and maybe someday, her mother.

Having a baby in her made it worse not to know where her mother was, and it made her even madder at Marlene for trusting jerk after jerk, for taking drink after drink.

When she got to Interstate 10, she turned west, toward the purple and red of the sky. Only one more road really to get to her father's. In Louisiana she would head north on Interstate 55. That would take her clear up into Illinois, not far from Half Moon. Two roads to get home. And she made a little tune to go with it: Two roads to go home.

5

When Ed and Janet and Nelson got to Edith's that evening, hoses were strung all around the yard, sprinkling what Edith apparently hoped would be a lawn, but Ed saw that she was just washing gullies in the topsoil and grass seed onto the hot cement. "Jannie," he said, "do you think it will take her as long to landscape this place as it's taking her to finish the lobby of the Half Moon?" Janet smiled, but there was a tiny blame in her glance and Ed realized he'd done it again. Edith *was* Janet's mother.

In this treeless yard, the sound and smell of water on hot cement and hot earth were the only reliefs from the heat. Ed wished he was back in town at the hotel under the cool old shade trees. The three of them watched the sprinklers and timed it so they could get to the front door only partly wet. "It's like jumping rope," said Janet and she ran on ahead. Nelson got thoroughly soaked because there was more of him to soak. Ed followed, and the water spattered loudly on his stiff pants.

The house, close with the smell of chicken baking, was quiet. They heard voices out back, so they went through to the living room, where the smell of hot chicken was combined with the smell of new carpet. Edith's furniture still had plastic covers on it—two reddish brown chairs and a peach-colored sofa. Janet went on out, pulling Nelson with her, but Ed stood at the patio door and looked out, hoping at that point he could some-how turn around and go home.

They were all there—their friends Ginny and Doc, Mary, Edith, Janet, and Nelson. They were out there standing in vines, squash vines, it looked like. Ed remem-bered Edith telling him something last winter about slip-ping on the ice at the construction site and spilling an aluminum pie plate of squash seeds. But what was she doing at a construction site with a pie plate of squash seeds? "Sprinklers in front," Ed muttered. "Squash vines in back, hot chicken on a hot day, no air-conditioning, and plastic-covered furniture. What a gal. A born hostess."

But they made a pretty picture out there, up to their calves in vines—Edith's friends and her daughters, who were Ed's friends and daughters, too. When Ed squinted they looked like some painting of a garden, their colors floating watery in the haze of heat against the dark green of the grove and vines. Ginny, tan and her silver hair shimmering, an orchid in that white sundress with the green sprigs on it. Doc, a stroke of light in the pale, crisp seersucker suit that Ed figured all country doctors should wear. Janet, in that pretty pink dress with her arms pale and her hair dark, seemed fragile, a moth against the green. Nelson was a long stem, a big stroke of pale blue paint above and dark blue below. And Mary, nearest to Ed, looked sturdy in an olive green dress with lacing at the waist. She lifted her wide, plain face to Ed and smiled. "How are you, Dad?" There was a little sweat on her upper lip and her reddish hair stuck to her forehead in a way Ed remembered from when she was a little girl. But now there was gray blurring the edges. For a moment Ed let himself see his red-haired oldest girl as the short, broadening middle-aged woman she was. "Fine, girlie, how are you?" and Ed stepped down into the backyard. How different she is from Janet. The world outside of her has not changed her face; she keeps what she thinks and feels so deep inside her that it's too far from her face to have any effect. Those who love her and have known her all her life know almost nothing about her. All that is known, though she lives here among them, is that her husband left twenty-five years ago, two weeks after they were married. Come to think of it, that was about all that has happened to her, except her garden in back of her little white house and all those Catholic masses. Daily masses for twenty-five years.

The heat.

Painted people in the squash vines. Patches of color. For a dream reason they were searching in the big prickly leaves. Edith, at the back door, called "Never mind! Never mind!" But they laughed and moved away from her like a slow herd of pastel, grazing cattle.

Ed took a step toward them out of the dream. They were picking zucchini no bigger than a thumb, and yellow squash blossoms. Edith had sent her guests out to pick squash for supper without realizing how small the squash were, and now, for revenge, they were picking them all. The sticky stems almost hobbled them. "No more!" called Edith. "No more!" Nelson stood up straight and waded through the vines over to Edith. He gave his handful of squash to her and turned to pass handfuls of squash from the others into the house. Ed watched. The heat. Someone handed him a cold drink.

Then they were all in the kitchen helping Edith with the salad and the zucchini. It turned out that anyone knew as much about Edith's kitchen as she did. The movers had put things away and, as Ed suspected, this was the first meal she had cooked in her new house. It was steamy and all Edith's new shiny surfaces were sticky with humidity. He couldn't help it; he asked her why she hadn't put in air-conditioning.

"I couldn't afford it!" she said, wildly scraping cucumbers over the sink. "Do you know how much that stuff costs? It costs . . . well, I don't remember the exact amount, but it is a lot!"

"Edith," he said, "you are a rich woman. You could air-condition the whole town with what you got from the land you sold to BuyMor. You're so rich you don't know what to do with your money." He wanted to know how much she'd gotten for the land; so did everyone else, probably, but Edith wasn't saying.

Edith was washing zucchini in the sink. Ed leaned on the refrigerator, and Doc and Nelson stood at the patio door that overlooked the big grove still left between here and the river. Ginny and Janet scraped carrots at the table. Mary walked around, quietly looking for dishes and silverware. It was nice, Ed thought, in this room full of people cooking supper.

"Look around you, Ed." Edith's arm with the paring knife took in the whole house. "Here's a lot of the money you want to know about. And I want to help out the girls. Maybe give some to the church." Mary took the knife out of her mother's hand—Edith didn't notice—and began to slice radishes.

Edith was sitting at the counter, staring out the window at the edge of the grove. She'd made herself a guest in her own home. Janet was getting dishes out. "Mom," she said, "why would you give money to St. Rose's? All you do is complain about it and the priests. You should be a Unitarian with Ginny and Doc."

"Or a vegetarian," Ed said under his breath.

Edith hove herself off the stool and turned to Janet. "Not be a Catholic? No novenas or midnight masses or candles or sodality or even processions? It would be too boring! They're all too boring, the Protestants." Ed was just about to start in again on the variety of Protestants when Janet asked Mary, "Do you still have sodality? I thought that went out with Vatican II."

"Maybe other places have it," Mary said, "but we don't here."

"The dud priests, that's why!" Edith was flaring up, but Janet was being reasonable.

"Mom, all you do is complain about the Catholic church. Do you even go?" She turned to Mary. "Does she go?"

Mary was reluctant to say. "You were there at Christmas and Easter, weren't you, Mom?"

"Of course I was there! The idea of joining another church!" she said to herself as she wiped dust off of plates with her apron.

Ed said, "Why don't you start a drama club instead? It would be less confusing."

Mary and Edith gave him looks.

"I guess not," Ed said, and with his toe, poked at a piece of zucchini on the floor. Mary picked up the zucchini and wiped at the invisible spot on the floor. Then Ed looked like he had another idea, "Or how about—"

"It's crowded in here, isn't it?" Edith drew herself up and made herself imposing in that way she had. Then it was crowded.

Ed headed for one of the doorways. "I was just looking for your toilet. This place isn't laid out like a normal house."

"It's not laid out like a ratty old farmhouse, you mean," Edith called after him. Ed wondered how many times in their lives he had left a room with Edith shouting after him.

When he came back, Janet had her hand on Edith's elbow to steer her to the stove. "The chickens are done, Mom. Should I put them on platters?"

Mary had finished up the green salad and taken a bowl of potato salad out of the refrigerator. "Mom," she said, "you forgot to cook the zucchini!"

Edith grasped the hair above her ears. "Zucchini?" she screamed. "It's the green beans I forgot! Fresh green beans were the whole reason for this party! I got them from one of my tenants south of town. A whole big bag of them! Just hours ago, they were picked! Hours! Where are they?" Ed stood out of the way and watched Edith frantically opening and closing cupboard doors and the refrigerator, looking for her bag of green beans. Then he quietly slipped out of the house. Shortly he came back with a big grocery sack. While Edith was again rummaging through the vegetable drawer, Ed reached into the sack and pulled out a handful of very limp green beans. "Is this what you were looking for?" It was a little mean, but it was fun.

"Where were they?" Edith was as limp as her beans.

"In the trunk of your car." They stood there a moment, the two of them, their eyes sending and receiving decades of old accusations.

"Let's eat," said Doc rubbing his hands. "We can always go to McDonald's later, if there isn't enough. Come on, Edith, my love." And Doc led Edith into the dining room, past Nelson, who had been watching all this from the doorway. He put out his arm and led Janet to the dining room. Ed followed with Ginny and Mary. "I've seen this in the movies," he said, steering the women through the narrow door to the dining room.

Ed thought it was like eating in a furniture store, and considered saying so. In that room were a new table, new chairs, new hutch, new sideboard—not a picture on the wall, not a plant, not a teacup or knicknack, not a sign of their former life together. But Ed kept his mouth shut and watched, between Nelson and Janet, the sun going down serene and red beyond the grove of oaks.

When Doc had carved the chicken—Edith wouldn't let Ed carve—and the food had been passed, there was a general discussion about what was the occasion for this dinner. Edith said of course it was Dr. Nelson Alvin's coming to town. "What about the green beans?" Ed asked. Before Edith could really start in on Ed, Ginny mentioned that today was the fifty-fifth anniversary of Doc's setting up practice in Half Moon. Mary, who usually doesn't volunteer, said there was another reason for the dinner and that was that Janet was back. Beers and gin-and-tonics were raised and Ed looked at his girls. Mary was trying to put some expression onto her face and Janet was trying to keep something off hers. "You didn't buy wine, Edith?" he asked, to cover their faces.

But Mary continued. "Jack is coming back too, and they are going to live here again." Mary looked at her mother, who nodded to confirm this.

There was a lot of cheering this time, but Janet, trying several times, interrupted. "Jack *might* come back, he *might*."

Then everyone put their glasses down and Janet's face was red.

Edith said, "You said Jack *was* coming back!"

"No, I didn't, Mom. I said he *might* come back. I said I had asked him to. He might."

"Well," said Edith breathlessly, "are you two *separated?*"

"Mom," Mary warned.

"He's not *here,*" said Janet and her arm took in the whole table, knocking over her glass.

She started to stand to wipe things up, but Edith put out her hand and held Janet at the table. "Forget that," she said.

For a moment Ed remembered why he had loved Edith: She doesn't give a damn about anything but the people she loves and she will do anything for you if she loves you.

"You and Jack aren't . . . breaking up, are you?" Edith had forgotten that anyone else was there.

Ginny said calmly, "Edith, maybe this isn't the place . . ."

"Of course it's the place," Edith said. She turned back to Janet. "Janet and Jack are our . . ." For once Edith was at a loss for words. She looked around the table. Janet was pale now, tears were in her eyes. "Jack and Janet are ours." She still had hold of Janet. "That's right, isn't it, Janet?"

Ed wanted to get Janet out of this, but all he could do was sit there.

Janet looked up and her eyes met Ed's while Edith insisted. "You're ours." Edith was right. He didn't want Jannie to go away again. He was old. He nodded.

Then Janet nodded. She could barely speak. "That's why I'm here. That's why I want him back here."

Edith smiled, relieved, as if everything were all settled. "Oh, honey!" she said. "We can manage that!"

Edith turned to Ed. Her yellow-brown eyes. She was right. Jack had to come home. Ed could see what Edith was thinking: Jack Hawn would have to come back to more than Janet. As good a girl as she is, a man like Jack has to come home for more reasons than love. He's got to come home for a job or for property or for both. With Edith's money, they would manage. Edith was right. The two of them would fix things for Janet.

Then everyone breathed again and began to pass food around.

Ed, passing potato salad to Doc at the head of the table, said, "Doc, did you hear the one about the two cannibals eating supper?"

"Christ, Ed!" said Edith, smiling now, "Do you have to?"

"Yup," said Ed.

"Go on," said Ginny, who loves jokes.

"See, these two cannibals were eating dinner and one says to the other, 'How's your mother-in-law?' 'Not too good.' So the first one says, 'Then just eat the noodles.'"

In the middle of all this, Janet had gotten up and gone in the kitchen for some dish towels to wipe up the spilled drink. When she came back in the dining room, Nelson, smiling and again in his courtly manner, stood up and carefully picked up the plates and silver and glasses in the pool of spilled drink. He wiped gin and tonic off Edith's new table.

Then, while the others were leaning over and arguing about the best way to remove the white alcohol stain from the walnut, Nelson turned, and Ed saw him delicately lift Janet's arm, wipe the spilled drink from her elbow and her forearm and her wrist, and then from each of her fingers one by one. Janet stood still while he did this, her face cast down, looking almost like the girl Janet standing in the yard while he, her father, dried her arms out by the pump.

Later, after supper, all of them except Doc, who sat in the yard and smoked one of his cigars, walked down to the grove and then to the river.

It was a dark night and close. Ed dropped back on the path. "Nelson, as far as the summers here go, you might as well have moved to Louisiana." Ed felt his voice muffled by the heavy air. He looked for stars or moon, but there was only the low pink glow from BuyMor across the river to guide them through the oaks and the brambles.

But in the grove they walked into cold air like floodwaters. The women walked ahead, light on their feet, their arms extended for coolness and for balance. Ed followed their pale dresses through the unaccustomed dark, while they followed Nelson's shirt—a high, pale rectangle like a window in the path ahead. Now and then one of them would stop, and standing still, listen to the pretty voices of the others going away, or listen to their own breathing, listen to the sounds of the grove—a breeze somewhere, a creaking branch, an owl, the rustling darkness—until fear caught at their ankles and they ran ahead. Now and then the women stopped and stood clumped close together so that, walking up to them, Ed could feel the heat of their bodies warm the air. He could, if he wanted, close his eyes and follow them by the trail of their warmth and the scents of their soap.

Now and then the women caught their dresses on brambles, and Nelson untangled them. They trusted his careful, useful hands. Ed watched as Nelson helped them over roots and, on the little bluff over the river, found them each dry places to sit. The women remarked on his night vision, and he said that was his gift—his ability to see in the dark. They said, oh no, you have other gifts too, you're kind and observant and helpful. They laughed and told him, "You're what we all wish all men were like." Nelson laughed and said, "My former wife would like to hear that." They said, "Former wife?" and, as the women sat on the bank with their feet hanging over the river, he told them about his divorce—enough so that Ginny put her arms around his broad back.

They sat on the little bluff a long time, mostly quiet. Ed stood behind them and listened for a trickle from the thick river, traced out the black trees against the blue-black sky and the pinkish glow across the river. The women's feet over the grassy bluff sometimes sent little rushes of dirt into the river, and now and then one of them threw a stick to find how far the darkness extended, how far into it she could reach.

Ed loved the women, and he watched over them until they finally got up and, laughing and scratched and bitten by mosquitoes, followed Nelson back to the glow of Edith's house.

6

Vickie was perched on a sawed-off telephone pole at the edge of the parking lot of a catfish restaurant in Vicksburg, Mississippi. It was nearly the end of June. She had been there early every morning for almost a week. At first she told the people who had asked what she was doing—the manager of the restaurant, and a cop, and the two women who came to clean the restaurant—that she was just looking at the river, she liked the river. But that hadn't seemed enough reason for them, so she told them she was a birdwatcher, but that a lot of people thought birdwatchers were crazy, that's why she didn't tell them right off. "Then where's your binoculars, honey?" one of the big cleaning women had asked. "Stolen out of my car in downtown Pensacola," she said. And then they'd talked about how you couldn't leave anything in your car anywhere these days and wasn't it a shame. "I don't remember when it wasn't like that," Vickie had told the women, and they felt bad for her youth. She told them her name was Lisa and that she'd heard from her mother who was also a birdwatcher that this was a real good place to come because there weren't many places where you could watch birds from above like you can there. One of the women said, that's right, this past spring she'd seen them V-shaped flocks of geese flying north right above the river. And then they'd all three stood there at the edge of the bluff and looked down a few moments at the treetops that the rising sun had not yet gotten to, below the bluffs of Vicksburg.

It was true. Besides the great bend in the brown river and the flat, forested land beyond, and the two bridges—one silver and one black—you could see birds flashing out of the dark forest below. And you could hear more birds than you could see; it was raucous down there, and it sounded like their singing was coming from inside a big room, out the windows of a room in which birdsong echoed. But now and then one or two would wheel up and over the treetops below and flash—no color that you could see, just silver like the river and the bridge. "Mighty pretty," one of the women had said and then they both sighed and went in to clean.

The next day, one of them brought her a pair of binoculars. "I got no use for them, baby, and my son don't nei-ther, where he's gone, so you take them." Then the two women looked at each other and Vickie could tell they had agreed on what they would say to her. The one who'd brought her the binoculars said, "It ain't none of my busi-ness, honey, but I'm going to say it anyway. Whatever trouble you're in, you just go on back to your people. They've got to understand. They're the ones who's got to understand." Vickie could see that they meant to be kind, but she didn't dare take it in. The other one said, "If you're expecting company pretty soon, you ought to be with your mama. Where is she, baby?" "I don't know," Vickie said. "Lord!" the woman said. "There's sure a lot of that going around—people lost their people. Or else you ain't telling us the truth." As they turned away, one of the women said to Vickie, "You could stay with us for a time, but even if this is the 1980s, it's still Mississippi."

She thought the binoculars might help her watch for her mother. It was the motel across the road from the restaurant that she was there to watch, not the birds. But when she put the binoculars up to her eyes and looked around, she became nauseated as she had been in the third month, and that was two months ago. She didn't know if looking for her mother was what got her out here so early in the morning or if she just couldn't stand the stale air in the car. As soon as there was a little bit of light, she would come out there. Even though she knew she wouldn't find her mother there now, it was the only place she knew to look. And she couldn't show up at her father's and say she hadn't looked for her mother.

Vicksburg was the last place she'd seen her mother and that was three years ago. It was an accident, their getting separated and Vickie hadn't believed that it would last; it couldn't. There had been a ruckus over at the motel, but she knew none of the people would remember her, if they were even the same people. Three years ago when she was sixteen she had been skinny and she had long straight light brown hair. Now she was still skinny in the arms and legs but all around the middle of her was thick and heavy, and her hair was blond and short and spiky. Or it was spiky when she had styling gel. In the drugstore in Pensacola she had everything she needed, but the idiot manager had cut Bo's credit card in half in front of her eyes. Those scissors had flashed right in front of her face like those birds down below and she could tell from the hate in the man's face that he wanted to cut her eyes out, so she called him a fucking asshole and left. Luckily, that time the car started right up. But she didn't have her styling gel or gas or anything else until she had worked a week at a Burger King outside of Mobile. Her food, what little she'd wanted, she got in the Burger King, and out back of there is where she had found the box that made sleeping in the car so much better. The car was a hatchback and the weather was warm, so she ought to have been comfortable before the box, but she was always waking up and someone was looking at her sleep or else she thought someone was and then she'd have to start the car and move. She chose places several times a night: She'd start out in a place that was lighted and safe, but someone always came and looked in. So she would find a dark place on a street or a road where no one could see in and watch her sleep, but then she couldn't sleep because she didn't know who or what was out there. One time possums had dropped onto the hood of her car from a tree and another time in a park she had looked out to see that the car was surrounded by little boys who were just watching her. But the worst time of all was the man who scratched and scratched at the door like a man in a horror movie, though she could tell from his eyes that he knew he would never get in. That didn't stop her from screaming. But nothing happened. He just wandered away. It was the homeless people who scared her most. You never knew who they might be or what they might do. Now she knew that the best place to sleep in your car was the parking lot of a small factory that had night shifts. There weren't usually guards or attendants in the lot, the cars were in the same shape as hers, and no one thought it was weird to see someone asleep in their car.

Now that she had the box she was fine at night, for the time being. She was pretty sure Bo didn't report the car as stolen right away because he wouldn't want to have to explain the bruise on her face, but just in case, she had taken the plates off and thrown them in a canal and at the Burger King she had taken some cardboard and a marker and made License Applied For signs instead of plates. The car was so old and in such bad shape she figured no one was going to give it much notice or make much of a fuss over it.

The box fit into the back of Bo's Toyota when the

backseat was down, and it was big enough to sleep in. Now at night she parked some place that looked safe; then, when she was sure no one was looking, she just crawled over the seat into the open end of the carton and went to sleep. It didn't look like a girl was sleeping in a car; it looked like somebody was hauling something. She hoped it didn't look like someone was hauling something valuable that someone would want to steal.

Vickie knew she had enough money for two more days, but she figured that it would take the police only one more day to get too curious about her being here in this parking lot every morning watching the birds down there and the motel across the street.

The Mississippi River below, the curve of it, was like music to Vickie; it was something that she should have nothing to do with until the baby was born because it caused her too much ache and made her lose her nerve when she looked south at where the river was going and north to where it had been.

Vickie had a lot to do before she could go to Half Moon where her father was. She knew that this would be a big thing for him, for anyone, to deal with—his nineteen-year-old daughter he probably wouldn't recognize showing up pregnant and single. Before she could get on Interstate 55 and drive north, she had made a list of things she had to do to make herself presentable to her father, to make the shock of all this a little easier to take:

— wait for bruise to clear up
— get 100 dollars in cash, plus gas money
— let roots grow out, cut off blond
— clean out car
— get two outfits and a suitcase
— think of new name and ones for the baby
— figure out story

Now and then she tried to tell herself that her father was an old man and she tried to picture him as an old man or even think of the real possibility that he was dead, but all she could do was see him at the farm and see herself as five or six watching him come into the back porch before supper and unbutton his coveralls and—he was always very tired—slowly step out of them. A cloud of dust always rose up and made her sneeze which made him laugh. Then there he was in the blue work clothes that had stayed clean under his coveralls, and she followed him into the bathroom where he washed his hands and face and the black dirt ran into the sink in little rivers. She couldn't really see his face. All she knew was that he was her father and he had loved her in the best way she had ever been loved and that as bad as things got with her mother, even when she was at her meanest and drunkest, she had always told Vickie that her father was a good man and that he loved her. But thinking like that caused the same ache as music and she looked down at the flashing birds over the forest and she could bear that sharpness much better than she could bear the slow curve of the river.

She was moving toward a picture in her head. She was using every ounce of energy and sense she had to carry herself toward making that picture real. The picture was a simple one, and one that was not filled in with any detail: It's the backyard of the farmhouse. She and her father sit on lawn chairs. The sun is going down. Sometimes in the picture the baby sits on her father's lap; sometimes it sits on hers. There are birds on the wires and in the trees.

She wants to get the eyes of the man in Pensacola with the scissors out of her mind. How could he hate her so much when he didn't even know her? Vickie was sure he would feel differently if he knew the story, but that was the problem: Most people did not want to hear your story. Or else if they did, how could you tell it, and what story could you tell when half the time you didn't know the right names for things? Like those birds. She didn't know the names of any of those birds though she was pretty sure that the loudest ones were blue jays.

Most of the time she knew people didn't want to hear what really happened. They wanted to know a story that made things easy on them—easy for them to hate you or easy for them to like you or use you or walk away. The real story was something that everybody was real careful to step around, real careful not to step in. She knew by now that all you had to do was give people a few hints and they would make up a story about you. She knew that waitresses, men in bars, kids—everyone who was first a stranger—would fill in the rest around your carefully chosen details, your first line. When a waitress would ask, "Where y'all from?" in response to her funny accent, Vickie would explain that she was an army brat and moved around a lot. Then she could watch the waitress's face as the story filled in behind it. When men in bars asked her why she was here all by herself, she always said she was there looking for her brother Jim who Mama was worried about. Did they know him? He had dark hair and was so tall and when he was drunk sometimes he would cry. They usually knew him, and then they always talked about themselves and each other and described the ways that they got drunk so that sometimes she picked out one who didn't hit people and lived close and was likely to pass out. She had gotten showers and a place to sleep that way. Before she had stopped going to high school, when she and her mother would get to a new place, she would just work out the few first lines that made her newness acceptable: My parents just got a divorce; my mother's company was moved here to

New Orleans; my mother was promoted—anything but my mother is a drunk who takes up with drunks and we always leave towns at night.

She had sent her father a few lines four or five times a year since she was a girl. A postcard or a valentine or Christmas card and on each one was enough to let him tell a pretty story to himself about her and her mother, Marlene. His address she could not forget because it was not really an address: Mr. Edward Check, R.R. #1, Half Moon, Illinois. Now and then she sent a photograph of herself, if she had one and if she liked it. Sometimes she put return addresses on the cards and sometimes she didn't, but return addresses didn't mean much to people who moved as much as she and her mother had. Only now and then over the years had a card or a birthday present from her father caught up with her. Calling him on the phone somehow didn't seem like the right thing to do.

The sun was now angling down into the forest below her so that when a bird would fly over the trees she could see the color of it. She wished she knew the names of the birds. She wished she could go down into that forest and stand in the middle of it with someone who knew the names of every bird and plant and tree, and that person would tell her all the names, tell her nothing but the names of things and she would remember them all. When she put the binoculars to her eyes, she saw some blue flash by, but she couldn't find it again and it made her sick to try to look.

She turned away from the forest and the river and looked at the motel across the street. She and her mother had come to Vicksburg that time three years ago because of the name of the town. Her mother had thought that would please her—going off the interstate out of their way just to stay in a town "that was named after you." They were on their way from New Orleans to Memphis.

They were leaving New Orleans because Marlene had broken up with her boyfriend, of course, and they were going to Memphis because that's where Marlene's sister was, with her new husband and her kids. "Your cousins," Marlene said to Vickie. Going to Vicksburg did please Vickie, more than she could let on, and she wished she had been interested enough in the new husband of her aunt to find out his last name so she could later on find them all.

Vickie had liked New Orleans and wanted to stay there, but her mother said no and Vickie came home from school one day to find their stuff packed and in the car and her mother standing by the car smoking. Not a word would she say except, "Get in," and that time Vickie had thrown a real fit, one that made the neighbors come to their windows and threaten Marlene. So Vickie got in the car and they left, but neither one spoke until they were in Vicksburg, and Vickie had asked, "What the fuck are we doing here? It's not on the way to Memphis!"

"This place was named after you. I wanted to have a look at it." Then Vickie hadn't wanted to, but she cried like a baby while they got off the interstate, and then her mother had pulled the car over right on the off ramp, and there at the edge of a field she had held Vickie in her arms while she cried like a baby, bawling and sniffling. Marlene had cried too.

They had checked into the motel across the way and then they'd taken baths and cleaned up and gone to dinner in the catfish restaurant. Looking over the silver bridge and the black one, Marlene said things would be different now. She would cut down on her drinking and they would have a fresh start. Everything felt fresh and clean and new for them after so much crying, and Vickie let herself believe her mother. But when they got back to the motel, Marlene had said she was going down the street just for a nightcap, just to get the highway jangles out of her arms.

Vickie didn't throw a fit this time. She just said, "Mother, if you walk out that door now, I won't be here when you get back." Marlene laughed. "I mean it," Vickie said.

"Maybe you do, but where would you go and with whose money?" And Marlene had left.

Then Vickie had gotten dressed again and walked toward the town and went into a pizza place, where she stood at the door a few minutes and looked at who was there. There were only three or four tables of people and one was a table of two high-school boys, so she walked over, pulled up a chair, and sat down. She smiled. They couldn't believe their luck.

Much of the rest of the night Vickie doesn't remember because of the drinking, but she woke up with one of those boys on a back porch in Jackson, Mississippi, and it took her two days to get someone to take her back to Vicksburg, and she couldn't call because she didn't remember the name of the motel. It was the Vicksburg Motel.

When she got back, her mother was gone. She had left the day before. Vickie had made a scene in the motel lobby. She insisted to the manager that her mother would have left word where she was going and that she wouldn't just leave her like this. "Where is the note?" she screamed into the man's face. "Where is the goddamned letter she left?"

The manager had just laughed at her tantrum while his wife called the police. "Listen here, Little Bit," he had said. "Why would I turn over some letter to you when she didn't turn over no money to me? We are both screwed by that bitch and you are probably better off without her. Go home to your daddy, who must be breathing easier with her out of the house." Vickie had gone for the man's face and was on top of him scratching at him and hammering with her fists when the police came and pulled her off.

They didn't put her in jail. They turned her over to some church people who said they could straighten her out, and five days later she was hitchhiking on the interstate. Then she was in Florida, where she met Bo.

She found out she was expecting for sure just as she and Bo were leaving the house one day to go to his sister's wedding. The phone rang and it was the clinic. She told Bo to go on to the car, she would be right there. He didn't know she'd gone to the clinic.

"Miss Vickie Chick?" the woman from the clinic said.

"Check," said Vickie.

"Miss Check, there is a pregnancy there. Is that good news or bad news?"

"We'll see," said Vickie. "Thanks."

She went to the wedding and nobody, not even Bo, could tell a thing was wrong. In those minutes after the phone call, Vickie felt herself change; she felt herself shut down one system and start up another one. She could almost hear it. She could feel the fierce little baby inside of her forcing Vickie to make a place for herself.

Sometimes at night when she was sleeping in the carton in the car, she cried for Calico, a cat they'd had on the farm when they still lived there with Papa. Because the box reminded her—the smell of the cardboard and her body's heat, the towels she slept on—she remembered very clearly Calico and her litter of kittens in the cardboard box on the porch. Vickie would lie next to them and put her face close to them. She could still remember the warm smell of the cats, like milk and dust, the squeaking of the kittens, the warm, warm sound of Calico purring as she nursed her blind babies with their sharp little claws like rats.

7

Janet and Ed were parked on the square, waiting for Nelson Alvin to come down from his office. It was six o'clock on a Friday evening in late June and the square was full of sun, empty of people. For a while they just sat looking out the open windows. Ed was working on sentences he might use to ask Janet what had happened between her and Carl years ago, but they were all too bald: Did you sleep with Carl the summer before you married his brother? Did you come back to see Carl? Is it over with you and Jack? He couldn't ask Janet anything like that. He turned to her and said, "We'll be late picking up Carl. Why don't you go up and find Nelson?"

"Why don't you?"

"You're too sassy, I'm too old, and he's your boss."

"He's your friend. You're the one who . . . picked him up. And besides, so far I've only worked for him for two days. And it's temporary. He's not my boss. Mom's my boss. I really work for her—until Deb can come back to work."

Ed wondered if working for Edith would be like living with Edith. "Don't say that," he said. He looked at Janet's hand, which rested on the gear-shift knob, to see what he could see there—Edith's hand or his own. He saw his mother's hand—not beautiful, but a kind, soft-skinned hand, now with the rivers of veins. He wondered if she could hear the currents of her own blood as he heard his own sometimes. What would it sound like to be Janet?

Janet didn't make a move to go upstairs for Nelson. She turned to Ed. "Did you go to the hospital to see Deb Whiteside?"

"I've been thinking about it, but I haven't decided whether she would want somebody to see her when she's been beat up by her son, or if she'd just as soon be left alone."

They sat silent another few minutes. "Poor Deb," said Ed. "What a terrible thing!"

"How badly was she hurt? All I heard was that the little jerk put her in the hospital." As Janet spoke, Ed saw under her eyes a shadow he'd seen in his mother's face, a kind of blue light from stretching herself too thin across some gap.

"He's a big jerk. She's got a broken jaw, two cracked ribs, a cracked wrist, and two broken fingers. Her typing fingers."

"They're all typing fingers."

"I guess you're right. Just not the way I would type."

As Janet got out of the car to go up and get him, Nelson came down the stairs. They could see him on the broad, steep stairway beyond the glass door. He came down fast, his feet a white blur on the dark stairs.

"He wears basketball shoes to work? An optometrist wears Nikes? I like that!" said Ed as he climbed in the backseat to make room for Nelson.

Nelson carried his jacket slung over his shoulder hooked on his thumb. He was whistling.

When Nelson got in the car, and the car tilted toward his side, Ed slid over behind Janet to balance things off, but there was no countertilt in Ed's direction. Nelson slammed the door, rattling Ed's teeth. Ed said, "How come you're so goddamned cheerful?"

"I love it here. You've got nice people here."

Janet said, "Dad, Nelson showed me how some of his equipment works today. He let me look at Nina Massey's retina. It looks like a map of rivers."

"Ed, come up sometime. I'll show you, if you're interested."

"Oh, I'm interested."

"I'm starved," said Janet. "Where are we going to eat?"

"I told you, Janet, that big steak place in Springfield with—"

"That great big place like a pole barn? The one they keep at forty-five degrees all year around? That place is still going? I haven't been there in . . . since before I was married."

"You don't like that place, we'll think of something else. We'll ask Carl. I bet he eats out a lot." Ed didn't want to go there either; he and Marlene used to go there. But that was the reason he'd suggested it.

"Yeah," Janet said. "But I don't know if we want to go to the places Carl frequents."

"Now tell me about this Carl," Nelson said as they left town and turned onto a country road. "Does he need glasses?"

"He might," said Ed, resting his arms on the backs of their front seats. "He needs something."

"We worry a little about Carl's drinking," Janet explained.

"I think you and some others overestimate Carl's drinking. I don't think it's as bad as all that," Ed said to Janet, wondering that she'd say this in front of Nelson.

"This Carl is an old friend of the family?" Nelson asked.

"Carl is . . . well, Carl is my son-in-law, Janet's brother-in-law for one thing. And we used to farm the land next to the Hawn's, so they were our neighbors for years."

"Now, I remember," Nelson said. "Carl is Jack's brother. And Carl is divorced, right?" Ed felt a small distaste for Nelson. He sounded like he was making out index cards on all the people in Half Moon. As if you just memorized everyone's name and a short history and you were in. Home free.

"Right. Shirley and the kids—those kids are grown now, that's hard to believe—they're still out in California, as far as I know," Ed told Nelson, in spite of himself. "I think she's remarried. The kids used to come out in the summer to see Carl, but they haven't been out in years. I think he misses them like crazy. I think that's Carl's problem, if he has one—missing his kids."

"Carl loved those kids, especially those little girls. I remember one time years ago going over to their place after supper and Carl was just sitting in the yard listening to his little kids upstairs playing while they took their baths. But, Dad, Carl was drinking a lot even in those days." Ed wished he had time to figure out the tones in her voice, the currents under the surface of it.

"What does Carl do?" Nelson asked.

Ed looked at Janet, who seemed to think telling Nelson anything was fine with her. "Do for a living?" he began. "Well, he still owns and farms the original eighty acres his great grandfather homesteaded in the 1870s." How could he tell this without tripping on the connections that still tied him to the place? "The Hawns, mainly D.E., Jack and Carl's dad, expanded to half a section and more to the north. Then when Edith Flaherty, your landlady"—he tapped Nelson on the shoulder—"sold her family's land—"

Janet interrupted him. "—the farm Dad and his family worked on from the beginning until about twenty years ago."

"—when she sold that farm, Carl—the bank, really—

bought it and then lost it when the economy fell apart and the banks chickened out. These guys, Nelson, guys your age and younger, were hundreds of thousands of dollars in hock to the banks. It was complicated, but with tractors costing sixty thousand dollars used, and the economy shifting on him, and his wife and kids taking off, and the booze, Carl gradually lost it all. But at least he still has the original eighty."

Ed stopped and watched some of the Hawn's old land pass the car window. Janet continued for him. "Eighty acres he can farm with a small tractor, four-row equipment, no hired help. So enough must come from that to support a bachelor with simple tastes." Ed was thinking that that and his own social security would be more than enough for him and Carl. He had an impulse to just move back out to the country and live with Carl in that big old house.

"Dad, do you think he drinks too much?" Janet asked, meeting his eye in the rearview mirror. Carl's drinking was an easier subject than who owns the farm.

"I admit he drinks a lot; maybe a lot is too much. It's changed. A lot is less than it used to be, and so is too much. To watch TV and read the papers, you'd think we were back in Prohibition. All some TV star has got to do to get free publicity and sympathy is to say he used to be a drunk. Sports guys, too. It's like some kind of trend. I just can't stand the reformed."

"Dad, what about Dale Whiteside, who put his mom in the hospital? Couldn't he stand a little reforming?"

"He could stand a little locking up and throwing away the key. That kid didn't punch out Deb just because he drinks; he did that because he is and always was a mean bastard, just like his rumored father."

"Who is his rumored father? It's not Dwayne Whiteside?"

"Never mind, honey. It's just rumors. And besides he's long gone and someone you barely know."

They drove along in silence for a while with all the windows down. The roadside buzzed with grasshoppers and crickets and when they turned onto the road past Hawns, a trail of dust followed them all the way to Carl's. This is where Ed came to get away from town, to get away from women who keep their arms too close to their bodies, from men who seem to be always so held in. He liked to be with Carl, because when Carl felt like hell, he looked like hell. If he didn't think something was worth doing, he didn't do it.

When they turned in the driveway, Ed couldn't wait to get out of the back of Janet's small car. Janet parked under the old, soft maple tree where everyone had always parked, and Ed pushed at the back of her seat. "Let me out, I'll go get him."

The back porch was close and rotten-smelling, hot; Carl hadn't taken down the storm windows on the porch. Ed knocked on the door and turned to speak to the black cat perched on the ledge when he saw Carl coming around the back of the house. Through the porch windows grimy with wind-blown field dirt, Ed thought Carl looked like the Carl of years ago—straight and lean and dressed neat. Ed stepped out on the back step with the cat in his arms. Carl stood at the bottom of the steps a moment, looking away, toward the car, hesitant. Carl's hair was damp and brushed back, out of his eyes, and his clothes were clean. He had a pair of pliers in his hand. But when Carl turned toward him, Ed could see how eroded was Carl's face.

"Hey, Ed, how you doing?" Carl was clearly glad to see Ed, but the cat jumped down and disappeared under the porch.

"You ready to go, Carl?"

"Well . . . come here a minute, OK?" Ed followed Carl around to the back of the house. "What do you think of this?" Carl pointed toward a charcoal grill with coals just about ready for cooking. There was also a cooler with ice and beer, some old lawn chairs Ed remembered from the old days, a card table with a cloth and a bowl and some plates on it. Carl looked at Ed. "Is this a good idea? Because nothing can't be undone. I can eat all this stuff later."

"It's a good idea, Carl. It's a good idea. Let's go get the others."

Janet and Nelson were standing by the car when Ed and Carl came around the house. "Jeez!" Carl said so only Ed could hear. "This guy's an optometrist? What a loss for basketball!"

A few minutes later they were all standing around the grill holding beers. Ed said, "Carl, I don't know if you know this, but there's cans of beans down in your charcoal."

"That's my invention. Why get a pan dirty when you can just do this?" Carl lifted off the grill and with the pliers shook one of the opened cans of beans heating down in the charcoal. Then he poked a finger into the other. "Just about done!" Carl looked up at the others watching him. "I do most of my cooking out here in the summer."

"What do you cook?" Janet asked him. Her words sounded careful and formal. She would keep a safe distance.

"Hamburgers. Hot dogs. About anything that won't fall through the cracks. Once I cooked a whole turkey breast on this thing." Ed couldn't hear a thing in Carl's voice that hinted at distance he had to keep.

"Was it good?"

"No, it was lousy. But I just didn't wait long enough for it to get done. I ate the done part, though. And the cats got the rest. They like it when I experiment. They think that's what I'm doing right now." Looking behind them, they all saw that there was an outer circle of cats, waiting, trying to look like it didn't matter to them whether they ate or not.

With the setting sun on the backs of their necks or their faces, they watched with infinite patience and interest the hot dogs and hamburgers sputter and burn. Your human being, Ed thought, is an odd beast. All that hustle and bustle and this is what makes him happy—some sun and some beer and meat and fire and a stick to poke in it.

When it was fully dark and the four of them had eaten Carl's hamburgers and hot dogs and beans, and thrown pieces of bread and meat to the cats, who now sat contented and random in the yard, Ed leaned back in a rusty old chair and watched the June bugs and moths swing in drunken ellipses around the gassy glow of the pole light. These kids were taking care of themselves. There was no combination of Carl and Janet he had to worry about; with Janet's carefulness and Carl's forgetting, there would be no veering off course. They could all be trusted to continue to talk about baseball and cars and music and car accidents and brands of beer for the rest of the evening. They were all a little drunk, but they would continue to circle each other as wide as the moths seemed to do.

It was late and they were listening to tapes of Merle Haggard and Hank Williams and Ray Charles on a boom box that Carl had propped in the kitchen window. Ed sat away from the others listening in the rusty chair against the wall of the garage with one of the big cats on his lap. The pole light cast the pattern of the maple tree like black lace onto Ed's face and shoulders, but the cat in his lap and his beer can and his hands were all silvery white. Now and then one of the three came out of the firelight— they'd dumped the coals on the ground and built a little bonfire—and brought him another beer or another cat, but with their music and fire and youth they were complete, and he was glad when they finally forgot he was there. He drank his beer and watched them against the white wall of the house under the dark windows.

Now they were acting like wild creatures who did not have middle-aged chins or crows' feet. They jumped up and, singly or in pairs, danced or swayed or ran away to pee in the orchard still singing, dancing all the way back. They danced with cats, who clawed their shoulders and jumped down into the dark. Now and then one of their faces would flare up above the fire.

Ed began to watch their shadows on the house behind them. The shadows twined and untwined and twisted and bowed and seemed to mock the bodies that sent them forth. Ed and the windows and the cats watched as first one man and the woman and then the other man and the woman danced a dance that seemed familiar to Ed, a dance that was the beginning of another dance, the beginning of an old story. It made him tired when he realized that he had seen pheasants in the field dance this dance, and cats, and all the animals. It was a mating dance, and for a moment his town temper flared, but he knew he might as well try to stop the wind. There was nothing he could or would do except see how it turned out, though at that moment he wasn't at all curious. He closed his eyes so as not to see the shadows dance, and the fire, the cold light of the pole light, and the dim light of the stars. He sat still in the chair, and gradually he let the music begin to dance him too.

Sweet dreams of you. They had put on a Patsy Cline tape and he almost got up to turn it off, the sudden memory of Marlene hurt so much. But he sat there and let her come and get him again—the strong, swelling woman's voice, with all her body's breaths and pride, her intelligence, her passion and beauty and pain, and now and then, her lies. "Sweet Dreams of You" and "Crazy" and "I

Fall to Pieces." Sweet dreams of you, oh sweet dreams of you. She had been in this yard many a time with him, and now he saw her walking after midnight in the orchard, then leaning into the smoke, and through one of the dark windows he saw her at the kitchen table, smoking a cigarette in the light of the little lamp. This was her voice that swelled in him and made all his skin remember the warmth and the heft of her curled naked next to him and he curved outside of her, even then, like a dry shell. She had been the meat of him, his heart and his muscle, and tonight all that was left of him was wanting her. How could she be gone? And why? And how could he bear it? How could he, a half-blind ugly old pisser, weather again such a storm of wanting? Ed couldn't swallow his beer and the tactless cat stood on his chest to sniff at the tears that dripped from his chin.

He pushed the cat off his lap and pulled himself to his feet. The others didn't see him disappear around the garage.

The spring she left there had been a storm, a wind storm, that here on this farm must have been a small tornado. He and Carl had spent a good part of the rest of the summer picking up the pieces of the tin roofs of the cribs and sheds that were laying all over the fields. The door of the barn had been wrenched off its track and though they'd put it back up, it had never really worked. He and Carl had left in place a souvenir of that storm—a branch of Osage orange driven by the wind into the side of the barn about five feet up. When they'd first found it, there were a few scraps of green leaves left on it. After Marlene had disappeared with little Vickie, Ed had not been able to say a word about their leaving to anyone, or to himself. The pain was something vast and indescribable that he was whirling inside of until he saw that branch rammed through the wall of the barn—by mere air. The sight of it was a relief, an odd explanation, a recognition that such things could happen other places in the world besides in his own chest.

In the dark, Ed stood leaning on the barn holding onto that branch, which was joined with the barn as tightly as it had been fifteen years ago. Out here the music was faint, and here there were no shadows, only a warm, sweet darkness that smelled like the grease and old hay and oats of the barn. Across the dark fields had been their house. The stars were faint in the thick, humid air. The footsteps beside him were that of a cat, who sat down and waited for whatever Ed would do next. He sighed. "I guess I'll survive, won't I?" he said to the cat. "I guess I don't have much choice."

Another step beside him was Carl, who sat down beside the cat. Ed sat down, too, on the tall fallen-over grass. They didn't speak. An owl flew out of the barn, making the cat duck. A plane crossed the sky, then a satellite. Another cat joined them. The music at the house had stopped. The grass grew cold. Finally Ed said, "Well, Carl?" And Carl helped him up and they went slowly back to the house, talking about how to fix the track on the door of the barn.

8

Think of it as play. Think of it as camping. Kids all the time want to sleep outside. Vickie remembered begging her mother to let her sleep out in the yard when they'd lived in New Orleans. She and Tula had dragged out blankets and pillows and slept in the grass behind the apartment building they lived in. Her mother said they could sleep out, but she had sat up on the balcony above them, watching. Vickie had seen the glow of her cigarette now and then and she'd heard the ice in her glass.

All it was was sleeping outside. The car was hot like an oven. What was the difference between sleeping in a car and sleeping beside a car? Sleeping on the ground was more natural than sleeping in a box in a car. Better. She'd sweated so much in the car that her cardboard box was collapsing with dampness and it stank.

If you went out there, was it better to make a lot of noise to scare things away or no noise at all so nothing or nobody would know you were there? Was it better to sleep where people could see you and know that there was a girl sleeping on the grass? Or was it better to sleep in the dark shadow of that bush by the courthouse over there so that anything that came across you was there by accident? Unless it was watching now. It. Or him. Or them.

Vickie stayed in the car and watched. And she listened to herself using up the air in the car.

Nothing moved anywhere. Bluish lights shined down on the empty parking lot. The outside of the spooky courthouse was lit with white lights hidden in the shrubbery. There was no moon. No stars. Just dark heat. Way down below was the glimmer of the river. If anything came up the hill to this building, she would see it come. Nothing moved in the bushes.

She woke in the car panting, soaked in sweat. In her dream her mother had been up on the courthouse balcony, smoking. Without jarring that picture of her mother, without looking up at the balcony, Vickie got out of the car. Air so heavy she could barely hear herself. Her mother watched over her, smoking and drinking up there. A gin-and-tonic. That's what she drank in New Orleans. Vickie spread one towel on the ground under the bushes and lay on it, and wadded up the other for a pillow. A leaf touched her hand and she touched it back. The leaf was warm and even the ground was warm. Down below in the town she heard cars. Then a train. But nothing made a sound here on this hill with her and her car and the courthouse.

It was a museum now, not a courthouse. It cost $1.50 for adults to go in, students grades 1 to 12 were 75 cents, and children under 6 were free. She had read the sign because there were no bathrooms outside and she wasn't sure she had enough gas in the car to get to the bathroom in the park outside of town. The man in the Hardee's had told her to buy something or not to come back.

In her mind's eye her mother up there behind her lit another cigarette. She smoked too much. Vickie told her, "Mom, you smoke too much."

In New Orleans, Vickie had been Kristi. Vickie came home from school and her mom was wearing the red-and-white waitress outfit Vickie hated. Was she going to work or just coming back? It was better if she didn't ask, so she sat down at the table next to her, close enough to smell that she just smelled like Mom, not like restaurant grease. So she would have to leave soon. "Mom, I'm going to be Kristi from now on." She spelled it for her.

"Jesus!" her mom had said. "Another new name? I was just getting used to Terri." Her mom had sat there and smoked and looked at Vickie. She was smiling and she looked at Vickie as if she could see everything there ever was to see in her. She looked at her as if Vickie was the most interesting thing in the world, and the most valuable. That look was like sun shining on her. "I can't keep up," her mom had said. "I'm just going to call you Honey Bee."

"Mother, I'm sixteen years old!"

"So how come you have to get born again each time you go to a new school? How come you have to get a new name like a baby?" Her mother smiled at her.

Then Vickie had ruined it. "How come we have to move every two weeks?" It had been her fault. She wanted to call those words back so her mom would sit there awhile, and smile on her like that. "Don't start again, Vickie." Her voice was hard and she got her purse and left.

That was the best place they lived, that last place. From the kitchen window you could look up and see the levee which was just a long grassy hill. Beyond it huge boats slid by on the river. You could just look up from washing a plate and a huge boat would slide by without a sound. A boat bigger than the building they lived in. And the air smelled good and yards were full of cats. She and her mother would sometimes take the ferry across the river to the French Quarter to walk around. She didn't remember what they looked at over there, but she sees as if from a high place Vickie and Marlene crossing a wide dusty lot near the ferry, the wind blowing into their faces, each shielding her eyes from the grit, hair and skirts blown back, holding hands.

She slept until morning when a car door slammed in the parking lot. Before the frowning woman got close enough to ask her questions, Vickie got in the car and left.

9

Ed drove over the noisy gravel in the parking lot of the state park below town and parked behind one of the telephone poles they'd laid down there to keep fools from driving onto the grass or into the river.

"I thought you didn't drive anymore," Edith said as he turned the car off and reached to unpack the fast-food lunch he'd brought along for them.

"I borrowed Janet's car," Ed said. His mind was elsewhere.

"I can see that! How's your arthritis? Let me see." And Edith took his right hand in hers, but he took it right back to hand her her turkey sandwich, unwrap his hot dog, put the straw in his root beer. "Ed," she continued as she chewed. "A man surely can't live long on hot dogs and root beer. Janet says that's all you eat."

"I'm almost eighty years old. What do you mean 'live long'?"

"Well, maybe you'd feel better if . . ."

". . . if I ate a tuna sandwich now and then? I don't think so, Edith."

"Suit yourself."

"Don't worry."

They both chewed for a while, inhaling the dust and heat, drinks in one hand, sandwiches in the other. Then

Edith said, "Let's go sit at one of those picnic tables and eat. It's cooler there."

"Bugs," said Ed.

"A farmer worried about bugs?"

"I'll work where there's bugs, but I don't want to eat among 'em." When he said that, Ed got a very clear picture of dead June bugs on the kitchen windowsill and the rug below the window at the house on the farm. He remembered the way those bugs hung on with the hooks on the ends of their legs when you tried to pick them off the rug—even though they were dead. And he could see, and could have reached out to touch, the kitchen window, its chipped green paint, the Virginia-creeper vine growing up the screen, the caulking around the sink, the green Formica counter and its metal edging. The vision was so real that when he rose out of it, he gasped.

"What's the matter with you, Ed?"

"Nothing. I was just trying to remember the names of those bugs like June bugs that came in the house each summer."

"Box-elder bugs?"

"No, no! These were those fat brown beetles like June bugs, only June bugs are as big as the end of your thumb and these were as big as the end of your little finger."

"Well, how the hell should I know? And why should you care?"

They ate in silence, both staring out at the family of geese on the muddy backwater of the Sugar River.

"Why'd you get me out here, Ed, if you're not going to talk? What's on your mind? You want to ask me to marry you again?" And Edith laughed hysterically, jouncing the car up and down, as she ate her French fries and drank her iced tea.

Ed stared in the side mirror watching two men behind them at the entrance to the park, apparently getting ready to dig holes to put up a new sign. There was a young fat one and a young skinny one. The fat one was saying, "The sons of bitches could of sharpened this sucker!" as he plunged the posthole digger down onto the dry hard sod. Must be clay, Ed thought; they should have brought one of those two-man augers. Up on the farm, the ground was usually not that hard, though it was hard in dry years. He remembered that feel of being jarred to your very core by the shock of the metal on iron-hard ground. He remembered the endlessness of the job of fencing a field, setting hundreds of Osage-orange posts into ground that didn't want them. Yet he would like to be back there with his father and grand-father figuring out how to get the goddamned job done with the least effort and the most talk. When he remem-bered the feel of a fence post in his hands, he also re-membered the disbelief he had felt when his dad told him that all this topsoil—loess—was blown in on the wind after the glaciers retreated, and that the clay and sand a few feet beneath it meant that all of this was one time at the bottom of an inland sea. He remembered Kenny's disbelief, too, and he thought of Kenny for the first time in maybe fifty years. Kenny was one of the crew that came up on the train from Pulaski County, Kentucky every year to pick corn when they still did it by hand. And for a few years Kenny would stay around and dig postholes until the ground froze. Kenny had red hair, said "piddle" instead of pillow, and never went to school ever. He ate peas with his knife and poured his coffee into the saucer to cool it off. Kenny was the one who told him about pussy.

Edith's voice was close to his ear. "You didn't even eat all your hot dog? What's eating you, Ed?"

"Nothing's eating me." Ed didn't remember what, but something was bothering him. It would come back to him, whatever it was. He looked at the overcast sky and the dried-up grass and the silted-in river.

The skinny one had taken the posthole digger out of the hands of the fat one. "Lyle, it ain't a cutter; it's a digger. And it don't dig *grass*. Get out of the way, now, and calm down." He was handling it all wrong, like it was a shovel with a lid. The fat one Ed didn't know, but the skinny one might be one of the Francises from over near Hull.

"Ed! Eat up! I got to get back to work." Ed couldn't remember why he'd asked her to have lunch with him. All he knew now was that her voice and her cologne didn't leave a person enough room to get anything up to your mouth. He handed her his unfinished lunch and his trash and she put them all together in the bag.

"Gimme that," Ed said and he got out of the car and carried it over to the trash can beyond the water fountain. Edith had gotten out and was brushing crumbs off the front of her bright green dress as she walked over to a bed of red cannas as tall as she was. Then she wobbled in her high heels across the lumpy grass and drank at the water fountain while Ed uncoiled a hose and fastened it to a spigot at the base of the fountain.

"Janet hates those flowers," Edith said, looking at the cannas. Squatting at the hose spigot, Ed looked up and saw her mouth above him—red and wet and dripping. "She calls them 'state-park flowers.' She says they're gaudy and trashy . . . I kind of like them myself."

"Figures," Ed said, still screwing on the hose.

"What are you doing, Ed? What's that for? Ed?"

Ed didn't answer. When the hose was fastened, he turned it on low, and with the trickle of water pointed away from himself, walked over to the two men trying to put up the post.

"Wet it," Ed said to them and laid the hose down so

the water ran onto the scratched ground they wanted to dig in.

"What?" they both said. They had stepped back, afraid of an old man coming toward them with a running hose.

"Wet it," Ed said again. "Let the hose run on it a while, then come back and dig. Or wait till tomorrow after it rains. Soften it up or bring an auger."

And then he walked back to the car where Edith was waiting. He'd remembered what it was. He went around to the passenger side and opened the door and took Edith by the elbow. "Come on," he said. "Let's sit over here by the river for a few minutes." And he steered her toward a picnic table under a scrawny walnut tree. They'd also used black walnut for fence posts now and then.

"I've got to go to work," Edith protested.

"Your money will be there when you get back. Just a few minutes."

Edith giggled. "You want to make out in the park like we used to?"

Ed didn't think that needed a reply, but he couldn't help himself. "We never made out in this park. You're thinking of one of your ugly old boyfriends."

"Maybe you're right." And Edith giggled again.

They both sat down at the picnic bench facing the river. Edith leaned back on the edge of the table and Ed leaned forward with his elbows resting on his knees. He rubbed his face with his fingers and palms like he was washing it, and then he sat up straight. "How does Janet seem to you?" he asked Edith, as if he knew the answer himself.

They were just suspicious, he told himself right after he'd said that. And he wished he could call it back, the opening of this Pandora's box. But he was not the one who opened it; this whole thing wasn't caused by his just asking about Janet. She and Nelson had opened it by . . .

by what? By acting crazy around a bonfire after drinking some beer? Acting like kids? No, it was more than that. Since then there had been looks back and forth between them, careful nonlooks, a vibration in voices, almost a smell in the air. It was *all* in the air; there was nothing you could nail down or call up as real evidence. And he tried again not to believe his own eyes and ears, tried again not to know what he knew he knew. Besides, what could he or anyone do? The only one who might be able to do anything was Jack. Jack had always been sure and decisive in his actions; he always seemed to look around and do the sensible thing, the thing that made the most sense for the most people. He wasn't like the rest of them; he didn't seem to choose for silly or selfish interests, out of nuttiness or whim or laziness. He had chosen to go to ag school because he thought the farm needed someone educated that way. He had chosen to marry Janet because it made so much sense and because he knew her and had always loved her. And after he had married Janet, and Marlene had married Ed, Jack had chosen to move out of the farmhouse and let Ed and Marlene live there because, with the baby coming, Ed and Marlene needed it the most. But the last thing he or anyone could do was call Jack and say, Come home, boy, to protect your interests.

Edith was talking—about Janet and how nice it was seeing her every day and what a good worker she was and how Nelson Alvin said the same. Ed stared at the river.

The problem with saying anything to Edith was that her response could go one of two ways—either she wouldn't know what the hell he was talking about or as soon as she did know, then the whole town knew and had to choose up sides. That was Ed's problem, he decided. He had chosen up sides and the side he had chosen was Jack's. Jack's and Janet's. They were a good couple—

though they had their problems — so he figured they belonged together. And he never had given up on that idea of Jack and Janet farming, living out there at the Hawn place with their kids. That picture of what had never happened was as real to him as his memories of driving Jack and Janet home from basketball games when they were kids, of taking them to the Farm Progress Show and wandering around with them eating those corn dogs and lemonade shake-ups, being as proud of Jack's brains and good looks as if he'd been Jack's father. It was too late, he supposed, but he still thought about Jack and Janet's babies, how they would seem to him doubly his, coming to him through Janet and through Jack.

"So Janet's just fine," Edith said. "Why do you ask? Is there something I don't know about?" But when Ed started to answer, Edith silenced him and went on. "You know, just before you picked me up, I finished up the paperwork on something for Janet and Jack. You don't realize it, of course, but I've been working like the devil at a way to get Jack to come back here. I figure a man like Jack is not coming to a place just because some woman wants him there, even if it is his home and she is my daughter. The girl just never was good at *working* men. She's as bad as Mary, almost." The look Ed sent Edith silenced her for a moment.

Ed said, "What do you mean? Paperwork on what?"

Then Ed watched Edith as she answered, and he could see that she hadn't the faintest idea of the effect on him of what she said. To Edith the events of twenty years ago were dead and buried; she had no idea what pain still lived like a spore-laden fungus under a thin layer of topsoil. The land that Edith had inherited from an aunt, the land that he and his father and grandfather had rented and broken and farmed, the land that Ed had been living on and, in his mind, saving for Jack and Janet to come back to, Edith had sold. Just before Janet and Jack decided to get married, Edith sold the farm. She broke Ed's lease and sold the farm. She did sell it to Carl Hawn, but she could have kept renting it to her own husband or she could have kept it for her own daughter. For years Ed had carefully avoided finding out who now owned that land. It was "just business," people would say, Edith would say, and he would say himself. But he walked out of any conversation where he might hear whose name was on the deed to the land he'd lived on for the first fifty-nine years of his life.

There in the park, Ed was beginning to feel sick — with resurfacing anger, with the confusion of dreams disappearing and dreams coming true, with the heat and the hot dogs. Now he was finding out. Edith owned the farm again. She actually had owned it for years. Now she was going to offer the lease to Jack.

"I've found another place for the guy who's renting it now," she said. She could have done this years ago. She could have offered the lease to Jack years ago. Or she could have offered the lease to him.

Ed stood and stepped toward the river. The sky was red, the river was red, as if he saw it all through the blood in his eyelids. His breaths were shallow and hot, hot and dry. He took another step toward the river, maybe his eyes were open, maybe they were shut, and then he whirled toward the sound of the water falling from the hose over there onto the dry ground, toward the voices of the men whose language he now didn't understand. For a long time he stepped blindly toward the voices, then when he felt the ground soft and muddy under his feet he sat down hard, right there in the cool. He was reaching out.

"Hey!" a man said. "Hey! What the hell?"

"Gimme the hose," Ed said in his own language. And

IDLE CURIOSITY

then it was in his hand and cold water was tumbling over
his hand and arm. Then it was on his head and the back
of his neck and dripping from his chin. The red was fad-
ing. The men were speaking English. So was Edith, who
was shaking his shoulder and speaking his name.

"I almost fainted," Ed said and smiled. He turned to
see Edith squatting beside him, real fear in her eyes. He
looked at her green high heels squishing up the mud,
and then he looked between her big knees clear up to
where he hadn't looked in . . . what? Thirty years? He
looked at Edith's face and then he addressed the darkness between her legs. "How long has it been, Edith?
Thirty years? Thirty-one?"

"Christ, Ed!" and she shoved at him and stood up. "I
was *worried* about you!"

"How long has it been?"

"He's out of his head!" she said to the two men.

"When was the very last time we did it? Do you remember? I think I do."

Edith was hauling him up. Ed was still holding onto
the hose and he was getting wetter and cooler. "You
know, I think it was one time when the girls were gone.
They must have been at school or maybe over at the
Hawns, but it was daytime." Edith was jerking him toward the car. He was forced to let go of the hose. "We'd
just eaten breakfast—pancakes, I think—and we went upstairs and just took off our clothes and rooted around all
morning."

Edith had opened the car door and shoved Ed into the
passenger seat.

"Remember that, Edith? That time you let me . . ."

"Just *shut up,* Ed. I'm taking you to the hospital."

"How come, Edith? Because I've got a hard-on? That
it? You're afraid I'm going to die from this hard-on? Don't
worry, it's not chronic. It's just a passing fancy." Now

Edith was driving fast to the hospital on the other side of town. She was running stop signs and taking corners too fast. "Let's don't waste it, Edith. Who knows? This might be my last great one. Look Edith! Ain't he a beauty." Edith wouldn't look down. When they pulled up in front of the hospital, Ed put his muddy hand on Edith's arm. "What are you going to tell them in there? That I almost fainted? You're going to tell them in the emergency room—where people die now and then—that you've brought in a man because he almost fainted in the heat? Or are you going to tell them about my hard-on?"

Edith's head rested on her arms on the steering wheel. She was sobbing, taking big gulps of air. Ed reached over and turned the key in the ignition. "Let's go," he said.

The emergency room's automatic doors opened, and a man in white came out. "Can I help you?" he said.

"False alarm," Ed said, smiling out the window. She's OK now. Aren't you, Edith?" She nodded. "She's just got to blow her nose and she'll be fine." Edith took the Kleenex that Ed had gotten out of her purse and she blew her nose. She put the car in gear and slowly drove Ed back to the hotel.

Later, in the cool evening, Ed was sitting out back of the hotel waiting for Nelson and Janet. He'd asked them to come out and have a beer with him, not out front "where all the old bastards sit," but there in back, where it was cooler and quieter. That space out back, the privacy, was, Ed figured, the only prerogative that came to him from being the former husband of the owner. They left him alone back here, and the chairs were his chairs. They were new plastic-covered wire chairs; he'd gotten them a few weeks ago at BuyMor, just after Nelson arrived. They were, amazingly, only $4.99. He had gotten a guy to help him move the stone bench to the corner of the yard nearest the hotel, and then he arranged the chairs around the bench like it was a table. You could put your feet up on the bench and you could put your chips and dip up there. He had put the other two chairs on the other side of the bench, where the light that was always on in the hallway would fall on their faces. When they got there.

They must have gone out to eat after work. He'd heard not a sound from either of their rooms and no lights were on, though he couldn't trust his hearing anymore. Even when he'd first moved in, he'd been able to hear pretty much who was home and who wasn't. But those days were gone. The world was getting quieter. "I guess I don't mind," he said to a sullen cat that crossed the yard without even giving him a look. "OK, don't even speak, you rotten bastard!" he added as the cat disappeared in the lilac bushes. High in the locust tree, a male cardinal was lit from behind by the setting sun so that he seemed to pulse like a heart. The female was a few feet below him, nervous and watchful. Then it occurred to Ed that because of the cat who'd just passed through, the cardinal was making that warning chip that cardinals make. He couldn't hear it, but he could see the bird pulsing silently open and shut.

The sun was leveling across the top of the room that was this yard, and the shafts of light through all the chaff and cottonwood fluff seemed to put a roof on it. The clearheaded feeling had stayed with him all afternoon and into the evening. All the craziness in the park was like a storm gone over, he said to the cardinal, and the air he saw through now was clearer than the air the cardinal looked through.

He remembered another time he'd gone to the park, right after the first time he'd gone out with Marlene. They'd had lunch together at her little apartment in town over the barbershop. She had to go back to work—she taught speed reading before and after school—but over their lunch they'd laughed and just talked like two adults who were evenly matched in both experience with loneliness and experience with jerks. And she was funny. He could still see her getting up to clear the plates and having to set them down to laugh at something he'd said. He could see her having to rest her two palms on the table to support herself through her laughing. He could still see the way she really looked at him through all their jokes, through all the cigarette smoke, and through the mire of what-will-people-think. After that lunch he knew that he loved her and, most surprising of all, he knew that she would love him. He'd driven out to the park and then on into the country to figure out what to do with this wonderful light-headedness, this sense of transformation, and this strange new fear. She was there and she was for him, but for how long? He had driven slowly down the middle of the road with both hands on the wheel and he laughed out loud, not really out of joy, but out of self-consciousness. He was stepping out of his own life. Up to that day he figured he knew the size and shape of the pain he expected to live with all his life. But now? Now he had no idea what form misery would take or from which direction it would come. He did know that driving down the road, he looked like an idiot—grinning and laughing and speeding up and slowing down, trailing his left arm out the window in the clean air, catching bugs. Ed could still see himself sweating, wiping his forehead with the back of his arm, pounding the steering wheel with his fist, steering with his knees, running both hands through his hair. He looked to himself—his hair stuck up in tufts, his expression was idiotic, his skin clammy—like the least romantic romantic lead on Planet Earth.

Then Ed saw through the near-dark that there in the

back of the hotel Janet sat in one of the chairs across from him. She had said something and was waiting for him to answer. She leaned toward him, her face warm and brown in the light, her arms brown, darker than her dress. "What did you say, Jannie? I was daydreaming."

"I just asked how you were, Dad." And she moved from the chair to sit on the bench closer to him, her knees at his knees. She took his hands in hers.

"I'm fine."

Janet moved back to the chair. "What did you say to Mom today? She came back to the office all upset. All she would say is 'Your father is a lunatic!' What is it that you did?"

"I guess I suggested the impossible." And Ed leaned down to get beers for each of them out of the little cooler beside his chair. "Don't worry, honey. I'm fine. You know how she overreacts." As he opened a beer for Janet he laughed to himself because Edith would never be able to tell that story to anyone. "How is it, working for your mother?"

"It's not bad actually. I never really knew much about what she did. I certainly didn't know how much property she owned. So it's interesting. And I'm finding out that actually she's only a real pain in the ass to us, to her family. To others, to her tenants and farmers, she's just a little flaky and scary."

"What do you do? What Deb did?"

"I guess so. I answer the phone and take messages and get her files and other stuff. Keep her appointments straight. Now and then type things. Nothing hard."

"But you're a nurse."

"I don't mind not being a nurse for a while. Besides, it gives me an opportunity to get to know Mom. And pretty soon, Deb Whiteside will want to come back to work. She's having a hard time getting over what Dale did to her."

"And do you type and do stuff for Nelson?"

"Pretty much." It was too dark for Ed to see if she blushed, but she took a sip of her beer and brushed imaginary hair out of her eyes. "That's interesting, too," she said.

"But for different reasons."

"Right." She looked up at Ed. "For different reasons. I get to take pictures of retinas and do glaucoma tests. And I'm getting to see lots of people I haven't seen since I was a kid. A lot of people are coming to him. People like him."

"I don't doubt it."

"And I think he's good."

"I expect he is."

"You like him, don't you, Dad?"

"Sure I like him, Kiddo." And he leaned forward and patted her hand. "I liked him first." She pulled back from him a little, confused. She doesn't know what he knows or what anyone knows anymore, or if it matters. For a few moments Ed watched her expression and saw her as the ten-year-old Janet. There was no way that she wouldn't be hurt somehow by all of this. He wanted to pick her up and carry her away from pain, but he didn't know any more than she did which direction it would be coming from. He was forming the sentence "I know what you're going through," but before he could speak it, he saw her face change as he heard Nelson come through the screen door behind him.

"Here he is." She got up and moved to the other chair.

Nelson squeezed Ed's shoulder as he passed him. "New chairs, Ed?" and Nelson sat down carefully.

Ed just shook his head as the little wire chair seemed to disappear beneath Nelson. "I don't know, Nel. I think if I were you I'd sit on the bench here. I should have thought of that when I got them."

Nelson got up and moved to the bench, and then he

pulled the cooler closer to him. "Do you mind?" he said, leaning toward the cooler.

"Not at all! Help yourself." Then while Nelson began telling about something that happened in the office that morning, something to do with lost contact lenses, Ed could see the consciousness their bodies had for each other, the unconscious parallel lines they made. It's an old story, he said to himself, married or unmarried, adulterous or not, and it's always the same story. He could tell it all to them now, though they haven't spoken a word of it to him.

Nelson was talking about a patient. Ed had lost the name and the line of the story, but it was pleasant to have Nelson talking to you. He didn't blame Janet. Nelson pays a kind of attention that Jack never could or did pay. In spite of all that heartiness, Jack is a pretty remote guy; he's always a long way away.

"Nelson," Ed asked, "how'd you get into that racket?"

Nelson laughed and swung one leg around so he straddled the bench. "Well, my father was an optometrist. An itinerant optometrist," he added, half to himself.

"Itinerant optometrist?" Ed said. "I didn't know there was such a thing."

"I mean he was temperamentally itinerant. Because he was such a son of a bitch, we moved around a lot. We had to move around. He was . . ." Nelson paused and leaned back, holding his arms around one knee. "He wasn't a very good optometrist, but worse than that, he was tactless, righteous, hostile, a son of a bitch with all the answers. Giving answers—whether or not you asked a question—was his calling; optometry was just a sideline."

Ed could see Janet's pale dress lean toward Nelson in the dark. "Why did you become an optometrist," she asked, "if you feel that way about him?"

"His work was always interesting to me. I spent a lot

of time with him, helping him out in the office. And—this will sound weird—it was clear to me when I was pretty young that he wasn't a very good optometrist and he was certainly horrible at human relations, so optometry was always work that I could see how to do well. Because of his bad example. Does that sound arrogant and horrible?" Nelson looked from one to the other.

"No, Nel," Ed told him. "It doesn't sound horrible. When I was a kid and I saw how sloppy and easygoing a farmer my father was, it embarrassed me. I swore I'd be a real go-getter of a farmer. Though, you know, when it came to it, I farmed just like he did. It's in the genes or something. Or else when you arrive at the same age and place as your father, it just makes sense to be what he was. But you're doing the opposite."

"I think I must be more like my mother. I don't think I ever felt like him. I mean, I don't recognize any of him in me, though that doesn't mean it isn't there."

"Where is it that you lived when you were a boy?" Janet asked.

"Oh, that was the hard part. We lived all over the place. Dad would get mad at somebody or some group of somebodies or else they would get mad at him, and we'd move. I hated that. That really is the main thing I've always wanted—to live in one place and to know I'll live there all the rest of my life."

Ed stood up and put his hand on Nelson's shoulder. "Maybe this will be the place." Ed knew that Janet would be thinking to say that, but it was better if he did. "Stay! Stay!" Ed said, as the two stood up to go in with him. "The night and you two are young and the beer is still cold."

Janet and Nelson, pretending a delicate obedience to Ed, stayed outside. From inside Ed looked back and saw them as still as two lawn ornaments that would come to life as soon as they knew they were invisible to human eyes.

How can I *not* want for Nelson, Ed wondered, what he wants for himself—to belong someplace and live there happily ever after. "If only their *belonging* wasn't right under my nose," he said out loud as he pushed open the door to his room. "And everyone else's."

By the time Ed got to his room and opened the windows, it had started to rain as he had known it would. "They *are* smart enough to come in out of the rain?" he said as he undressed for bed. As he touched his head to the pillow and turned his head to the faint sound and smell of the rain, he remembered a time years ago when he was coming back to the house, out of the field, because it had started to rain. He drove the truck into the driveway, and the three children who had been playing in the front yard—his Janet and the two Hawn boys—ran like mad, hollering all the way, to hide behind the house. They were playing some game in the rain to scare themselves. Mary came out to meet him on the step, wiping her hands on her apron like the lady of the house. After Ed washed up, she gave him a cup of coffee and a slice of warm banana bread she'd made herself. Edith came clattering down from upstairs in her mules and, passing through the dining room, went to the back door and called Janet. "Get in here and brush your hair! Come in out of the rain!" Edith came back and flopped down across from him at the table, blowing her bangs away from her eyes. She had a hairbrush in her hand and a couple of little blue barrettes.

They must have talked about something while they waited for Janet. Mary must have been there, Edith must have had a cup of coffee, too, but Ed remembered none of that.

What he remembered next was Edith holding Janet's

skinny body between her knees, Edith brushing and braiding Janet's thick and tangled hair. And he saw the solemn, twelve-year-old Jack Hawn standing with his arms folded, just inside the doorway, watching. In a few minutes Jack reached around into the kitchen and jerked his giggling little brother into the room, holding Carl in front of him with his arms around Carl's neck. It was odd how silent and content they all were watching Janet's hair being brushed and braided.

10

Last night Vickie slept in her car. For three days she had been sleeping in the car in this same pretty neighborhood below the old courthouse where there were lots of big old houses and bushes in bloom and birds singing. In the daytime the neighborhood was crowded with tour buses and cars full of ladies touring the antebellum homes, but at night it was quiet there and Vickie felt safe inside the box in the car, though the word "antebellum" made her nervous. She had seen the signs for "Tours of Antebellum Homes" and wondered what it was those ladies were anti. Yet in that neighborhood she felt safe leaving the car windows down a little for the fresh air and the sounds of the breeze. Since she was quiet and was careful to draw no attention to herself, she was sure no one had noticed her. But she was running out of money and food. She would have to find work soon.

When she woke up that morning and looked out the car window at the big house she was parked in front of, Vickie saw the curtains move. She saw a dark hand put a sign in the window: "Household Help Wanted." The sign hadn't been there yesterday, and she figured she would have a good chance for the job if she got there early. So Vickie drove fast to the Burger King, where she hurriedly washed her face and brushed her teeth, then she drove back to the house, parked in front, and went right up the wide brick steps and knocked on the door. Her bright blue sweatpants and T-shirt would have to do. The hand took the sign out of the window, then the door opened, and Vickie walked in.

The big cool dark space confused her. The two women—one white and one black—confused her. Usually Vickie sized up people and places fast and moved fast with her story, but these women looked at her with sharp dark eyes that kept Vickie silent. Then they looked at each other. Without saying a word, the tall, black woman asked a question and the short, plump white woman answered. Go ahead as planned, the look said. Then Vickie knew they had been talking about her, about *her,* they had been waiting for *her.* The sign was put in the window to get her in the antebellum house. This was a trap she had guarded against for years—disappearing inside somebody's weird fantasy.

She couldn't get her breath and her legs were turning to jelly. Keeping her eyes on the women, she began to back toward the door, her shoes squeaking on the black and white marble. She reached behind her for the big doorknob as the women both reached out toward her. Behind her back, she tried to turn the knob, but her hand was weak and sweaty. "No!" she said, as she collapsed on the marble tile. She put her head between her knees and covered the back of her head with her clasped hands. "No," she said again, but her voice was muffled by her legs, the cloth of her sweatpants. The women knelt beside her, one on each side of her. One patted her hands; one rubbed her back. "Lisa," the white woman said, "don't be afraid. We're not going to hurt you. We want to help you, Lisa."

"Lisa?" Vickie was silent. She looked up. There was a polished dark wood staircase curving up to the second floor, a beautiful curve.

Suddenly she was overwhelmingly tired and heavy. Heavy and sleepy. "How do you know my name?" she asked the staircase. "Veda and Odell told us." The black woman was speaking.

Vickie turned toward her. "Who . . . ?"

"You talked to them—the women who clean Catfish America—the restaurant."

Vickie didn't ask the next question, but the white woman answered it, all of them still crouching there by the door. "We need some help and so do you. There's just the two of us taking care of this house this summer and it is clear you should not be alone and sleeping in your car. In a cardboard box in your car."

Vickie put her head back down on her knees. She could sleep right here, right now. She closed her eyes. The women stood up. Vickie felt herself pulled to her feet. Under her arms she was wet and she hoped the women couldn't smell her sweat and her dirty hair and clothes. She opened her eyes and took a deep breath and, feeling heavy and old, walked with the women across the wide entryway with a floor like a checkerboard, past the gleaming staircase, down a long hall into a big white kitchen full of sunlight and the smell of toast and bacon.

There was a long scarred wooden table and at one end of it three places were set. "Sit down, Lisa," one of them said, and Vickie sat down. The white woman sat beside her. The black woman opened a big oven door that shrieked and took out three plates warming there and then a teapot. She set a plate at each place and then she sat down across from them. Vickie looked down at the plate in front of her: grits and bacon and eggs—bright and beautiful like a painting. She felt her tears start up again and she covered her face. "Do you drink tea, honey?" one of them asked. Vickie nodded. As she wiped her eyes, she saw a teacup placed before her in the sun and the tea tilting there formed shimmering amber ovals, and honey in a crystal jar as pretty as a crown of gold. The woman beside her picked up the white cloth beside the fork, unfolded it, and put it into her lap. Vickie did the same. The woman beside her put her hand on Vickie's. Vickie saw that she wore a gold wedding ring and another ring with a red stone. The sun shined into the woman's transparent white skin. There were many colors there to see, beautiful green and blue and purple and red under the skin. Vickie almost couldn't pull her eyes away to pick up her fork. The woman had spoken. "You eat something first, and then we'll talk."

The silverware was heavy. Vickie was embarrassed at the saliva that formed when she picked up her fork. She had no idea how hungry she was.

The three of them ate silently, the two women watching to see that Vickie ate enough, offering her more. After breakfast was finished, and the black woman was clearing the dishes, the white woman said to Vickie, "We'll bring our tea in here," and she got up, carrying her teacup. Vickie picked up her teacup and followed her into a little room crowded with big furniture—sofa, chairs, television set—just off the kitchen. The windows were full of plants—Vickie didn't know what kind—but still the sun came through to make more leaf patterns on the red and blue leaf patterns of the rug. Vickie and the white woman sat on the sofa and soon the black woman came in carrying her tea, and she sat down in one of the big chairs.

"First of all," the white woman said, "I am Mrs. Phillipa Merton and this is Mrs. Mavis Sloan. You are Lisa, is that right?" Vickie nodded. "And what is your family name, Lisa?"

"Check," she said and she spelled it for them.

"Why don't you just go ahead and call us Phillipa and

Mavis, since there's just the three of us here. 'Mrs. Merton' and 'Mrs. Sloan' just takes too much time." Mavis Sloan nodded.

Vickie said, "And you just call me Lisa."

The two women looked at each other and then composed their faces and nodded solemnly at Vickie.

Mrs. Phillipa Merton continued. "Due to certain financial reversals," she smiled grimly at Mrs. Mavis Sloan, "there are only two of us here for the summer to keep things shipshape for the guests and for the private parties. As you can see, this is a big house, so we can use some light housekeeping help." She paused and thought a moment. Mavis Sloan looked at her encouragingly and then Phillipa Merton went on. "And it is clear to us that you could use some help, too." Vickie was aware that both of the women made an effort not to look at her belly. "So what we propose is what you would call a trade." Mavis Sloan nodded. "We will give you room and board and a small allowance a week and we will see that our friend, Dr. Sand, looks after you if you need it. And you work for us here in the house until October doing mainly dusting and polishing and other light cleaning." She paused and looked at Mavis Sloan and they nodded at each other. And then she turned to Vickie, "How does that sound to you?"

Vickie wanted to ask them how *much* allowance and where would she sleep and does "board" mean food, but she merely said that it sounded fine to her. And she waited for them to ask about her baby—when it was due or who was its father or what were her plans or where was her family—but they didn't ask. They stood up and she stood up and Phillipa Merton said that Mavis would show her to her room.

Vickie followed Mavis's dark blue skirt up a dark, narrow stairway at the back of the house. Vickie's room would be a little one on the third floor over the kitchen. In it were a single bed with a white spread, a dresser, and a little chair with a faded blue slipcover on it. "The bathroom is this way, down the hall," Mavis told her and Vickie followed her to a white-tiled room almost as big as her bedroom where the old bathtub was almost as big as a bed. Mavis saw her eyes light up at the sight of the tub. "Honey, let's go down and get your stuff and then you can spend all afternoon in that tub, if you want. We won't make you start work until tomorrow. There's a washer and dryer in the basement. We can wash up your clothes today, too."

Then she and Mavis went to her car and both of them got in; Mavis was going to show Vickie where to park it in the back so it would be off the street and not in the way of the ladies on tour. "Besides," Mavis said, "it isn't exactly a beauty. These people don't like to be reminded of such things." When Vickie saw that Mavis meant for her to park the car inside an old garage next to two other cars—a dark blue expensive one and a rusted-out version of the same thing, she giggled. "Why are you laughing?" Mavis asked as they got out of the car in the darkness speckled with sunbeams and the rustle and coo of pigeons.

"My boyfriend would never find me or the car here. It's a hiding place like in the movies."

"This his car? Is he from the state of 'License Applied For'?"

"It's his car, but . . ."

"I know that 'but.' That 'but' means this is all you ever got from him and all you're ever gonna get and it's a hell of a lot less than you deserve. Is that right?"

"That's right." Vickie glanced warily at Mavis as she stuffed her few possessions—another pair of pants, a T-shirt, several towels, some cheap underwear, motel shampoo and soap—into the plastic garbage bag she'd taken from the Burger King back in Mobile.

"You're traveling a little light, aren't you, Missy?"

"I always do," said Vickie.

"I bet you do," Mavis said smiling as they went through a little door of the big garage—it looked like it used to be a stable—into a walled brick garden.

"Mavis!" The voice floated down through the thick leaves of a magnolia and they could see Phillipa Merton dimly in a second-story window, beyond a screen. "Mavis, remember what I told you!"

Mavis and Vickie were halfway down the outside stairs to the cellar, when Mavis turned back. "I almost forgot." And Mavis smiled at Vickie.

Under her breath she said, "I got to do this. Just don't *worry* about it."

And she took the bag of clothes out of Vickie's hand and went out to the middle of the garden. Then she pulled over a galvanized washtub and a hose and filled up the tub and then dumped all of Vickie's possessions into it.

Vickie felt her breathing get shallow and the hair on the back of her neck prickle. Facing away from the dim figure in the window she asked Mavis, "Why are you doing that?"

"Cockroaches and fleas," Mavis said. "She's afraid all the homeless got cockroaches and fleas."

"I'm not *homeless*! I don't have *bugs*! I'm going home to my father in Illinois!" Vickie felt her indignation almost raise her off the ground.

Mavis stood up straight. "Then why don't we just save everyone a lot of trouble. Go on in and call him and have him come and get you or send you some money." Mavis was watching Vickie's face.

"I can't go home like *this*."

"If you can't go home like that, it ain't no home to you.

And, face it, you're homeless. You and about a million others."

"I'm not! I hate the—*Men* and *winos* are homeless!"

"Oh, honey! I'm not saying it's anything you *did*. It's something that *happened* to you." Mavis was stirring the tub of clothes with the handle of a broom. They both stood over it, as if they were making soup, Vickie shivering and hugging herself though the air was steamy. Mavis continued, staring into the tub, "Do you know why there is so many homeless?"

Vickie shook her head.

Mavis snapped out, "Because there isn't enough homes."

Vickie watched Mavis's face, wondering if Mavis thought that was smart or funny or some big truth. And she wondered why Mavis hadn't asked her all the questions that strangers always ask—where are you from and where are you going and what is your story, because now that she'd eaten again, she was ready with a story. She was going to use the one about her mother being in the military.

"And do you know why there isn't enough homes?"

Again Vickie shook her head.

"Because men are two kinds of scum!"

Vickie smiled. "What are the two kinds?"

"I'm glad you asked that."

The voice floated down through the trees again. "Find any?"

Mavis called back without changing the expression on her face, "Not a one. She's a clean girl." Then she squatted down and started wringing out Vickie's clothes. Before she put them back in the garbage bag, she lifted it with the broom handle and turned it inside out and shook it. Mrs. Phillipa Merton wasn't the only one who thought Vickie might have bugs.

"I'm glad you asked that," Mavis repeated. "A girl like you can't hear this too often or too early." She looked at Vickie's belly. "Though in your case it looks like too little and too late."

Again the voice came out of the trees. "The dressing gown is on the washer, Mavis. And her clean things are up by the tub."

"All right, Phillipa." Then, to Vickie, "Down here, honey."

And Vickie followed Mavis down into the damp cellar where a washer and dryer were lined up right next to an old wringer washer, which was next to a pair of washtubs. Mavis dumped Vickie's clothes right into the washer and put in soap and turned it on hot and started it up. Then she handed Vickie the bathrobe that was on the washer. "Strip," she said.

Vickie didn't move; she didn't understand. Mavis was impatient. "Take your clothes off, so we can throw them in the wash! All of them."

Vickie dodged around Mavis and headed up the cellar stairs. Mavis's voice followed her. "The garage door is locked. And everything you own except the dirty clothes on your back is in that washer."

Vickie faced her on the stairs. "Are you out of your fucking mind? Do you think I'm going to take my clothes off in front of a person I've known a total of about an hour?"

"You've done it plenty of times in front of *men* you've known less time than that. And baby, you're a lot safer taking your clothes off in front of me than any man." She took a step toward Vickie on the stairs. "And let me tell you something. Don't you ever use that *'fucking'* language around Phillipa Merton, because if you do, that sweet southern lady will just tear your head off. And you will have lost this opportunity. And believe me, it *is* an opportunity. You need this. You need a roof over your head and a bed to sleep in and a couple of smart women to look after you and boss you around. You may think you know a lot because you've survived this long out there, but you don't know shit. You have not survived in a world this evil as long as I have and you do not know what I know and what even Mrs. Phillipa Merton knows. She is a rich and white Southern woman, but she is still a woman in a man's world and she can teach the likes of you a thing or two." She threw the bathrobe over Vickie's shoulder. "Now take your clothes off and put them dirty ones in the washer. Then we'll go upstairs and you'll take a nice hot bath for as long as you like and then when you come downstairs we'll eat some ice cream." She smiled at Vickie. "It might be strange being here, but nobody is going to hurt you."

After supper Mavis and Vickie were sitting in the room off the kitchen watching television. They were eating more ice cream. Vickie had taken a long hot bath and washed her hair three times with the shampoo they had put out for her. Then she had put on the maternity outfit that was hanging on the back of the bathroom door. It was a pretty brown and green leaf-printed top and skirt that felt good against Vickie's skin. "This sure is heavy cotton," Vickie had said to Phillipa. "Why, honey, that's linen," Mrs. Merton had told her. Vickie had seen 1950s things like this in secondhand clothing stores, but she had never been able to afford them. Mrs. Phillipa Merton had told her that she wore these maternity clothes before her son Montgomery was born. ("That Montgomery is a prick," Mavis told Vickie later as she showed her the house. "If he shows up, don't ever let yourself be alone in a room with him.") Vickie didn't have any styling gel, so she could not do anything interesting with her hair—

she knew spiking it wouldn't be the thing to do here anyway—so she just combed it back and let it dry naturally into a wavy, two-colored ducktail. Another three or four weeks and she would be able to get the blond tips trimmed off, and her hair would be back to its natural light brown. She had been a blond as a baby, though, and wondered if the thing to do for her father was to dye it all blond again. Maybe not, because the light brown was the same as her mother's.

Vickie finished her mint chocolate-chip ice cream and took her bowl and Mavis's out to the kitchen and rinsed them and put them in the dishwasher. In her bare feet and with the linen cloth on her body, she felt the beautiful, rich, big house all around her and she felt the food filling her belly. She would sleep high up in a house and between sheets tonight. She was smiling when she went back into the little sitting room.

"Mavis," she said, "you didn't get a chance to finish telling me about the two kinds of scum that men are."

"That's right, I didn't. Well . . ." and Mavis slipped her shoes off and pushed back in the recliner so that the leg rest came up. "The two kinds are the kind that is there and the kind that is not there. If a man stays around and lives in a house with you or if you have to work with him, then he is the kind who knows everything and tells you what to do and how to do it, only he's more than half the time wrong. Or he wants to get in your pants and he's otherwise all over you. The kind that's there, you wish would go away. The other kind is the kind that is never there when you need him or when he has some responsibility he ought to be taking care of. In my experience all men can be lumped into one of those two groups, and they can shift from one group to another. All that really changes is where they're at."

Smoothing the linen cloth on her thighs, Vickie said, "I think that is true of all the men I've known except my father."

"It's true of him, too." Mavis was flipping from channel to channel with the remote control.

"He's a good man. I know it."

"Well, where is he?" Mavis turned and looked at her. "I mean where is he when you need him? Not here! When was the last time you saw him?"

Vickie looked at the television and didn't answer.

"When? When was it? When did he send you money or presents or call you up?" Vickie wouldn't look at her. She couldn't think of a story to tell about him. She'd never been able to make up anything about him. Mavis reached over and shook Vickie's wrist. "When?" she insisted.

Vickie looked at her hand and then turned to her. "I haven't seen Papa since I was six years old."

"See what I mean?" Mavis said triumphantly. "Even your daddy is one kind of scum."

Vickie couldn't stop herself. "Maybe it's possible that some women are just always in the wrong place at the wrong time. Maybe everything isn't the man's fault!"

Mavis cocked her head and looked at Vickie, squinting her eyes. "You're not stupid, are you." It wasn't a question.

"No, I'm not!" and Vickie smiled and so did Mavis and then they watched *Dallas*.

When a commercial came on, Vickie asked Mavis where Mrs. Merton was. "Will she come sit with us?"

Mavis snorted. "Nighttime separates the men from the boys, and it separates the black from the white. She will be nice as you please, we will be as equal as you please all day long, then as soon as it's dark, she is upstairs in her 'parlor' listening to the radio and writing little notes at her spindly legged desk, and we are down here setting on the worst furniture, watching the old TV. She put it down here when she got a new one."

"Mavis, *I'm* not black."

"I noticed that. But to her you are poor white—not exactly trash, but not up to her station."

"Then why does she have me here? Why am I wearing her old maternity clothes?"

"Because you're her project this summer. It makes her feel good. And because she needs you. You're even cheaper help than I am."

Deep inside of Vickie, something fluttered. It was something that she'd never felt before, something she knew she had no control over. She tilted her head to listen, picturing as she did the robins listening for the life under the grass.

"What is it, Lisa? Are you all right?" Mavis swung her feet over the edge of the recliner.

"I just felt something," Vickie said, putting her hand on her belly. "It wasn't like anything else."

"Did it hurt?"

"No."

"Have you ever felt this before?"

"No." She was moving her hand around on the fine cloth.

"About how far along are you?"

"About five months."

"Well, that's the quickening, honey. You're feeling your baby kick you for the first time, or bang his little hand on you. That's the quickening."

"Is it normal?"

"It sure is! As normal as apple pie! I can see I've got a lot to tell you. What are you going to name this little thing?"

Up to that moment Vickie didn't know, but when she spoke, she was sure. "If it's a boy, I'll name him 'Edward,' after my father. Who isn't scum!"

"All right, honey. And if it's a girl?"

"I'll name her 'Cornelia.'"

"That's pretty. That's real pretty. I like that. But why 'Cornelia'?"

"Because in the Vicksburg Public Library a few days ago, I was looking in a name book and I saw that part of the word 'Cornelia' meant 'strength and courage and curved like the arms of a river.' I just like the sound of the word and the sound of its meaning. What do you think, Mavis?"

"I think it's pretty, too, honey. Very pretty. Let's just hope it's a girl so you can name her Cornelia."

Later that night, looking at the moonlight gleam on the tiny piece of the Mississippi River that she could see from her window, Vickie spoke to her baby for the first time. "Cornelia, I think we have a place to live."

11

The pounding of his chest woke Ed up. In his dream it was little fists knocking, knocking on his ribs, knocking to be let in. When he figured he was mostly awake, he fumbled for his glasses and turned to the digital clock. 2:37 A.M. The red glow of the clock lit the postcard on the table by the couch. Ed picked it up and held it lightly over the spot where the pounding came from. "From inside, not outside, you fool," he said to himself. This had happened before. If he lay still, it went away. It didn't hurt; it was just like moving fast and staying put at the same time, but it made him sweat. He lay there trying to think of everything but the motion in his chest. When it stopped, he would get up and change his pajamas, since these were sweated through. Or maybe he should just get up and put his clothes on. Then what would he do until the café opened at six? The pounding was subsiding. He looked at the picture on the postcard, which he could just make out by the glow of the clock. It was a long postcard with a panorama view of the oxbow curve of the Mississippi River at Vicksburg, down in Mississippi. The river was big, he'd forgotten how big. And the land across the river was as flat as here. What state was that across the river? Louisiana? Vickie was in Mississippi, or she had been, in the middle of July—the thirteenth, to be exact. That's what the postmark said.

Several times a year since she was a little girl, she had sent him postcards from places in the South. Pretty places, but all different places. Never a phone number, only sometimes a return address. Until six months ago they had come from New Orleans for over a year. Florida. Now Vicksburg. He had been to Vicksburg once when he was a young man—with Kenny, his dad's hired hand. They were on their way to New Orleans; Kenny wanted to show Ed New Orleans, but it turned out that New Orleans was just whorehouses to Kenny. Ed wanted to look around at the buildings and listen to the different ways people talked down there. On that trip Ed realized that he was pretty good at striking up conversations with strangers and that he wasn't as obsessed with the idea of getting laid as he had up to that point believed. Vicksburg had been a pleasant, sleepy place as he remembered, with big old houses slowly falling down and with the river down below to remind those people all day long of the passing of time.

Vickie had been in Vicksburg. She said on the back of the postcard, "This is a pretty town, one of the prettiest we've ever been to." She never said who "we" was; maybe it was Marlene, but Vickie never said. "I'm doing fine, better than a long time." All those previous "doing fines" he had tried to believe in, but couldn't. Maybe this one was something he could believe. What he knew from the postcards was that she was alive, she was in the South, and she thought of him sometimes. "You would like the scenery here," she continued in her careful, neat, girl's handwriting. "You would like all the birds. Love, Your Daughter, Vickie." This one had no small, elaborate story about being a cheerleader, having a boyfriend with a Mustang, having a "really, really good job." He might have believed those little stories if the postcards came from the same place, but it was clear that she or "they" were on the move, and he couldn't read that as good news. Probably this was the only gift she could give him right now—pretty lies to believe about her so he would not worry. But he worried. There was so much that could happen to girls. And to women. Dreams of what could happen—to Vickie, and to Mary and Janet and Marlene—were what started that pounding in his chest, dreams that usually only seeped out at night. And in all the dreams he was helpless to save them—mired in something awful or tied to something heavy or too far away or mute.

The pounding was gone now, but it was 3:04 and Ed was wide awake and sticky in the damp pajamas and sheets. He sat up slowly. Still quiet inside his ribs. He put his feet on the floor. So far so good. He stood and he was not dizzy. He went to the sink and ate a peach. He felt pretty good. He washed a little and dressed slowly, putting on pants and a shirt and his shoes. He felt fine. He left his room, quietly closing the door behind him.

Standing on the porch of the hotel, he saw that he was the only human being in sight, though a big, hump-backed raccoon slunk across the street just out of the pool of one of the streetlights. The air was fresh and clean on his face. It soothed him, eased the tense muscles in his face and neck and back. It reminded him that they all were in it, in the good air that he figured was what the Catholics got mixed up with grace. His daughters could do this too—go out into the night air or the fresh morning air and be . . . what? Be washed in it. Ed said softly, "Now I'm thinking like a Baptist." And he laughed and went down the steps and began to walk through his town.

After a couple of blocks, he passed St. Rose's, where he saw through the leaded windows that a blue light burned inside, probably a candle in blue glass, but it looked like a TV set from here. Maybe Father Grady keeps the TV going in some modern kind of vigil. Ed rehearsed what he would say the next time he saw the priest. "Say, Father, I see you're keeping the TV on in church at night. Bishop Sheen reruns? Pope specials? Tapes of old ladies saying the rosary?" He thought maybe he would ask him if the prayers counted as much in reruns as they did live. But that might be pushing him too far.

A raccoon or dog rattled the hedge between Mary's and the rectory. He wished she'd get a real fence, not just all those bushes. He remembered wild dogs in the country in the old days and thought it was something you couldn't be too careful about. The country was just down at the end of the street. Mary had left a light on in the kitchen. Another of her careless housekeeping habits. If you could call it housekeeping. Still, he didn't worry about her. She was set in her safe ways. And right under Edith's sometimes useful thumb.

Janet was out from under Edith's thumb because Deb Whiteside was well enough to go back to work typing one-handed for Edith and Nelson. So Janet wasn't working and she hadn't said anything about what she was going to do. As far as he could tell, she was doing nothing. She slept too late and she looked pale, but she and Mary were doing a little bit of work in Edith's new yard, and now and then Janet would help Mary in her garden — she still liked to dig in the dirt. About half the time, Ed thought Janet should take a job at the hospital to help Jack out when he took Edith up on her offer.

Her offer. He was Janet's father, but he had no offer to make, he had no decisions to make. He didn't even really know what to wish for Janet. Should he wish for her a marriage that made sense in so many ways and at least gave her a kind of stability? They've been together all their lives, Janet and Jack; could thirty more years kill them? Or should he wish for Janet the kind of insane happiness with Nelson that he'd had with Marlene? Should she choose, as he did finally, with her dumb blood and her tired heart? She might have no choice, really. How could she *not* go back to Jack if it meant they together would finally get a farm? Staying with Nelson would be forcing Jack out of a choice. Ed didn't think Janet could do that to Jack. He was sure she wouldn't. "Goddamn you, Edith!" he swore in the dense darkness under a black maple. If the farm were his, he knew there would be all sorts of kinder and crazier offers he could make. He'd give the farm to Janet directly or offer the lease to her or to all three of his girls. But Edith could only make it be a great big carrot to dangle like a big stick in front of the failing marriage of Janet and Jack.

Halfway down the hill, Ed stopped in front of a little tan brick house with a big picture window in the front. One of the Foster sisters still lived there, but he couldn't remember which one. The living room was all lit up so the picture window floated in the dark street like a big movie screen. "Well, looky there," Ed said. "It's Jesus on the big screen." On the wall opposite the window was a big picture of Jesus over Miss Foster's sofa. Lights shined on the picture from above and below and the drapes were left open so that whoever passed in the night could stop to contemplate Jesus. Jesus, a long-haired blond with a neatly trimmed beard, sat on a hillside in his white robe with his hands on his knees. Though behind him was a great full moon rising above some cyprus trees and some rocky blue hills, Jesus had more important things to think about. "Well, so do I," Ed said to the painting. "But it's still nice to be out on a night like this, wouldn't you say?"

Ed walked on down the hill. "Look," he said to Jesus,

whom he didn't believe in. "If you decide to show up in a place like this, I would get a haircut and shave and a good suit. Not too good, though. A brown suit. No sandals. And speak right up. Don't act strange. They don't like their saviors different around here." At the bottom of the street he turned the corner onto Edge Street whose houses faced the corn and bean fields. "But a savior would have to act strange. The idea of saving, as far as I can tell, is to shake people up so they let go of their ordinary bad habits, so they see something besides the day-to-day way to live."

A few blocks down Edge Street was Deb Whiteside's little house, just like the Fosters' only her picture window was dark. Ed had heard that Deb would always have trouble with the wrist that had been broken by that bastard, her son. Hers and Jim Starr's bastard son, Ed was pretty sure, though he didn't see any good in saying so. He figured Jim Starr left Mary when he found out that Deb Whiteside was pregnant with his kid. Some prize he turned out to be. There was some kind of restraining order to keep the kid away from Deb, but Ed knew it would take an electric fence. Ed stood a moment under a maple tree looking at Deb's darkened house when he heard the side door open. Then he saw the unmistakable figure of Nelson Alvin come out of her house and disappear into the alley. He heard Nelson's Volkswagen start up, and then he heard it drive away.

While Ed stood in the deep darkness of the tree, an engine in him seemed to start up—his breath and the pounding of his blood—and his vision seemed taken up by the shifting of some nightmare machinery, a tilting and grinding around him and under his feet. He turned on his heel and walked blindly to the end of the street and into a bean field. He walked straight down the row until the pounding died down in his ears, until his sight cleared and his breathing quieted, and he could feel under his feet the familiar warm and cooling earth.

Then he stopped. He was well out in the field. When his breathing slowed, he could hear the dry leaves and pods of the beans patter gently around him. It was a familiar and friendly sound. He sat down on the ground, which was quilted with the pale, dry, heart-shaped bean leaves. The leaves were damp, but when Ed brushed them away, the earth beneath still held the stored warmth of the day. He sat down to think. What difference had knowing this made? What did he know? What he did know was that for a long confused moment he didn't know who was in that house that Nelson was coming out of. He had thought Marlene was in there. Or was it Janet? Or Edith? And where was he?

He was sleepy. A breeze picked up and the bean pods clattered. Ed reached out and pulled one of the pods off the vine. He shelled it, unconsciously putting a bean in his mouth to test it for moisture. "About ready," he said of the field of beans as he lay back with his head resting on the furrow. He slept until dawn.

Ed woke up knowing what to do.

He went back to the Half Moon and cleaned himself up. He put on a jacket and tie. He called Edith. He woke her up, he could hear it in her voice, though she denied it. "Edith, put the coffee on. I'm coming over. This is important."

"Christ!" she said, but he could tell that she was curious.

Then he went up to Janet's room and knocked on the door. "It's your dad," he said and after a moment or two she let him in. She didn't look so good, even for a person who had just woken up. "Sit down a minute," he said to her.

"Why are you all dressed up, Dad?"

"I need two things. I need your car keys. And I need you to tell me something."

"What's going on? What's happened?" Ed could see that she was frightened at his odd behavior. But it looked like she was more scared of something else. He pulled up a little chair and sat down with his knees right at her knees. He took her hands in his. "Can I use your car," he said, "just to go out to your mother's for a few minutes?"

"Let me drive you, Dad."

"No, I need to go by myself."

"Sure, if driving won't hurt your hands, if you need to go."

"I need to."

They sat still a moment. Ed could see past her into her future, a future without a husband to fight with or eat with or sleep with. He knew much better than she the toll that loneliness, that having no place of your own, could take. He knew better than she that maybe even more than love, all they could really give each other was time, days and nights and years together. "Jannie, what do you want? Whatever it is, I will help you get it. Who do you want to be with? Jack or Nelson?" Janet gasped and pulled away from him. "Listen, kid, I've known all along. I'm not shocked, I'm not—I know how you feel. I think I do. I'm your father, but I know how you feel."

She stared at him, tears rolling down her cheeks, which bore the marks of the pillow.

"They're both good men," he said, taking her hands again. "They both have their faults, but they're both good men."

"I don't know if I have a choice," Janet said, so quietly that Ed almost couldn't hear her. "Nelson is seeing someone else."

"I know, but we don't know what that means right now. It could mean something and it could mean nothing.

We do know that the time you've had with him could be a place to start. A place to start for years to come."

It was clear to Ed that at that moment Janet could say nothing. She didn't have enough information. Neither did he.

"Where's your keys?" She pointed to the bureau. He got up and grabbed the keys, accidentally grabbing the lace doily too, pulling everything on the bureau onto the floor. Ed stopped. The two of them looked at each other and laughed. He quickly went to the bathroom for a washcloth, wet it, wrung it out, came out and gently washed his daughter's face. "I gotta go," he said, handing her the washcloth. "You're not in this alone, remember." And he went out the back way and took Janet's car to Edith's.

Ed parked in Edith's driveway and went around back. He figured she would be sitting at the kitchen table in her bathrobe trying to wake up. That's where she was. He knocked on the patio door. She waved him in. He slid the screen door open as she poured him a cup of coffee. She pointed to the chair opposite her and Ed sat down in it.

"How many cups have you had?" Ed asked her. She held up one finger. Ed sat back to wait. Edith, before her third cup, was not someone you would want to deal with. They sat in silence, looking at the woods behind the house, the mist that rose among the trees. Ed felt his breast pocket. The postcard of the Mississippi River was there, folded in half.

Finally Edith turned and looked at Ed. The coffee had put the intelligence back in her eyes. "Where are you going in that outfit? Is there some funeral I don't know about?"

"Nowhere but here," Ed said, answering her first question.

Edith, hearing him answer the second, was irate.

"What the hell do you mean by that? I don't want any of your bullshit this hour in the morning. I don't want you coming over here working your bullshit on me. I've got plenty on my mind that you do not have on yours, and I don't need anything from you except that you speak your piece." She was leaning across the table and tapping his hand sharply when she needed a little extra business behind a particular word. "And remember, what I appreciate is brevity and candor."

"You know, Edith, it's taken me about sixty years—I guess I'm a slow learner—but I've finally figured out what you mean by candor. Candor in a person is them giving *you* the opportunity to say whatever it is *you* want to say." He had come here to ask Edith to marry him again. But they were back in the fray.

"That's exactly the kind of crap I don't need," she said, and she got up and went to the patio door. She was wearing a long orange robe that zipped all the way down the front. It bothered Ed that she had clothes in her closet that he had never seen.

"Here I am," she continued in a whine, "worried sick about my daughter and you come over and give me this kind of shit!"

"I'm worried, too," Ed said.

"You! You don't worry!"

"I worry."

"You do not. You do *nothing*. You tell jokes and stories and you just watch what goes on all around you and not a soul knows what you really think about a thing. I mean the world could come down around your ears—and maybe it is even as we speak—and you just watch. Oh, you *talk*, I know that. But I know you well enough to know that your talk is just a way to find out about people, and a smoke screen for your goddamned curiosity."

Edith stopped to get her breath. Ed watched her with his hands on his knees. He had pushed his chair back from the table.

In a slightly quieter voice she went on, as if to placate him. "I always told people, when they asked how I could leave such a nice man as Ed Check, that the man had only one quality, and that a woman has to live with someone who has at least two or three. But you have just the one."

"For the record, Edith, what is the one?"

"Curiosity," she said. "Idle curiosity. Nothing happens because of it."

Ed stood up. "All kinds of shit happens because of your evil mouth! And you are as blind as a bat, Edith. The qualities, as you say, that you need in a man are stone deafness, a hell of a thick hide, and balls that are already numb!"

Ed left in a blind rage.

The blood was still pounding in his ears when he went to the café and sat at the end of the counter—not at the table with all the regulars where he always sat. There was a lot of uproar, not only because Ed didn't sit with them, but because he was wearing a jacket and tie, but Ed waved them away and the color of his face told them to leave him alone. He drank his coffee and ate his eggs and bacon and hashbrowns without even noticing which one it was who waited on him, or finding out a single detail of her life.

When he left the café, Ed forgot he had Janet's car. He walked, as he always did, to the post office to get his mail from the post-office box. Among the usual flyers was another postcard from Vickie. This one, too, was from Vicksburg, Mississippi. "Dear Dad," it said, "I love watching the river from my room on the back of this beautiful house. Some day I would like you to come for a visit. Love, Your Daughter, Vickie." It was addressed to him at Rural Route 1, as all the rest of them had been.

The picture on the postcard was of a big house, a bed-and-breakfast it said. The address was printed very small under the picture.

He went to the phone booth outside the post office. He put in the quarter, after trying a nickel, and called Carl.

"You want to go for a ride?" he asked Carl.

"Where to?" asked Carl.

"Vicksburg, Mississippi."

There was a pause. Then Carl said, "I suppose you've got a good reason for going there."

"I do. Do you have a vehicle that will make it there?"

"And back?"

"And back."

"The truck," Carl said. "Do you have gas money?"

"Yeah," Ed said, reaching for his wallet.

"When do you want to leave?" asked Carl.

"Have you had breakfast?"

"That soon?"

"That soon."

"Where are you?"

"Pick me up in back of the hotel."

"OK. I'll be there in about twenty minutes."

"Thanks, Carl."

"You bet."

It wasn't until they got to Cairo, Illinois, that Ed Check regained enough composure to tell Carl that they were going to get Vickie.

"What about Marlene?" Carl asked.

"I don't know about Marlene," Ed said.

12

This morning again Vickie was out early, before anyone was up. Pretty soon Mavis and Vickie would fix breakfast to carry up to the guests in the fancy bedrooms, bedrooms that would smell like bad breath when you carried in the coffee and the tray with shirred eggs and biscuits and roses.

Vickie helped Phillipa tend the herbs that grew in one of the sunny patches in the yard. In her bare feet she was mindful of the bees and sweetgum balls. Like the bees, her favorites were the oregano and thyme—the pale purple blooms and the scent crushed under her feet and into her palms. Not long ago she had thought of oregano only as green flakes you shake out of a little jar. And she had never smelled thyme or tarragon.

Here in the garden, with scissors and a basket with a handle, she was a girl in a storybook coming out of a big house to gather roses and dill. Seven roses, one for each guest room, one for Mrs. Phillipa Merton's tray, one for Mavis and one for her. Creamy apricot roses. Last week she picked one and before she knew what she was doing, she took a bite right out of it. The yellow roses smelled like sugared iced tea. Perfect white ones reminded her of saints. The red ones made her arms ache with some want she couldn't name.

Wading into the still-wet herbs, she stopped. A big fat

garden spider had woven her web across the row and hung there as heavy as a ripe cherry in her dewy web in the center of her life, the delicate lines sent out farther than her arms were long. Vickie squatted until her knees ached, inches from the spider's red eyes, bloodthirsty for a moth's dumb flutter into the trap. And then, right in front of her face, a fly fumbled into the edge of the web and the message was sent on the wires. In a second the spider was there spinning the caught fly, turning and turning with all her thumbs, wrapping it as neat as the butcher in the market tying the butcher paper with the twine. Vickie stood and laughed and went around to the fence to cut the dill.

She filled the basket with the dill's heavy yellow heads and feathery leaves as the first blue jays shrilled in the magnolia. She smiled, smelling the air fresh before cars drove around in it, feeling it cool before the sun heated it and swelled her legs and feet. The breeze cooled the back of her neck; she moved slowly to make it last, but when she heard the screen door open, she speeded up her lazy arms and legs. Without looking she knew it was Mavis, coming to see what was taking her so long.

She smiled, knowing Mavis wouldn't call to her because that would wake up one of the northern guests. These people were from Illinois, from Chicago. She didn't think of Illinois anymore; she didn't think of going to her father or his farm. This was where she wanted to stay. This was what they called an historic house.

Mrs. Phillipa Merton had shelves of books about historic houses. Phillipa, and Mavis too, had told her stories about this house and the War Between the States and about the awful General Grant—a man from Illinois, they pointed out—and the Siege of Vicksburg, about General Pemberton and the terrible summer of 1863. They told her about the caves and how the women and children had to go live in caves in the side of the hills and how these beautiful houses were shelled by the Yankees and some were used as hospitals. When Vickie heard about the shelling of the houses, she was not on the side of the Northerners, and they said many of the Northerners were from Illinois.

Vickie would sit in the rocker in Mrs. Merton's parlor and rest one of the big books on what was left of her lap and look at the pictures of the historic houses all over the country. None of these houses were in Illinois, she noticed. There were lots of Mississippi houses in those books. But her favorite house in all the books was one in Richmond, Virginia. It was a house called Wilton. All these houses had names like people did.

Wilton was a big house that looked to Vickie just like houses ought to look. The dark green door was in the center of the front of the brick house and over the top was a nice triangle-shaped decoration. There were two windows with little panes on either side of the door and on the second floor there were five windows so the middle one was right over the door. It was all so symmetrical; it was a house that she could draw. And she did draw it on some paper that Mrs. Merton gave her. She drew the house and its four big chimneys and the straight brick walk up to the front door. It was solid and square and neat, not as fancy as most of the houses in the books, but one that did not confuse you with curves and curlicues and decorations.

All those houses—here in Vicksburg, too. So many houses all over the place. How could there not be a house for her? She used to ask her mother that. "Honey," she'd say, "you get a house the way you get everything— with money."

"But still," Vickie would say to her mother or say to herself, "there are so many houses. Why isn't there one, single, particular place for us?"

Vickie now saw that all her mother's moving from city to city had been bringing her here to this house in Vicksburg. It was clear that here was where she was meant to be. There was the name of the town for one thing. And this is where her mother disappeared. All those stories she read as a girl, all those fairy tales of lost girls and big houses. From the distance and height of this house Vickie could see the pale traces of the paths she'd followed over the years to bring her here—from Illinois, to Memphis with that horrible Donald her mother liked for a while, then to Dallas and Jim Starr who was even worse, Houston and two guys there, New Orleans and more boyfriends. But these boyfriends of her mother's Vickie now saw as some kind of dumb princes who could not help but lead her to this place. And Bo was her own dumb prince. He got her the baby, and the baby got her here. The baby was the weight that would keep her here.

But she didn't feel heavy. She was light on her feet— until the evenings, when she was tired. She was strong. She had energy. She was smiling when she carried the dill and the roses into the kitchen. Mavis smiled too. It was one of Mavis's good days, Vickie could tell.

"Girl," she said, "walk over to Pearl's Market and get two good heads of lettuce. Don't forget to pick off the brown leaves before she weighs them. But don't let her catch you at it."

13

Ed knew it was a hospital room, but where? The ceiling was white and the walls pale blue. There was a window, but all it showed was a piece of blue sky in the morning someplace. The window faced west; that much he knew. The light had something in it that the light at home did not have. He didn't know what, but he would figure it out. It was important to figure it out. He knew he was high up in this building, but he didn't know how he knew it.

His glasses. He hoped they were in that bedside table that he could not reach. He wondered if he was in pain. No. It didn't seem like it. He tried out his arms and legs and they worked. But he was very tired. And weak. Too tired almost to think about where he was and when.

Time had busted loose from the holding ratchet that had kept him at the present, so he had backslid into the past somewhere or slipped on into the future. But where and how far? He was hooked up to other lines than time. He was hooked up to what must be a heart-monitor thing and he was hooked up to an IV line going into his arm and another line going out of him down there over the side of the bed. That was enough to know for now.

When he woke the sun was on this side of the building and it was still the same day as it was awhile ago. He felt a little stronger. He tried out his voice. "Where the hell are you, Ed? What the hell has happened to you now?"

His voice worked OK, but he could tell he hadn't used it for a while and his throat was sore. He was thirsty. There was a turquoise plastic pitcher on a table over the bed and a plastic cup all wrapped in plastic like in motels. If he could sit up and drink a glass of water, then he would be OK. If this were a hospital, really, then there would be one of those deals that you use to move the bed up and down. He felt around. Another line. He pulled on it and there were the controls in his hand. Arrows on it. He held the controls close to his face and pushed one of the arrows. His feet went up. Another arrow. There. His head was going up; he was being bent in the middle and then his eyes were higher than the pitcher of water on the table at his knees. He hoped it was water. He lifted it. Maybe it was heavy water. Lead. He lifted the glass. He tore at the plastic, but it didn't rip. He tried to bite it. But his teeth were someplace else. His pocketknife. He felt for the knife in his pants' pockets, but of course, no pants. In his shirt pocket. No shirt. But it felt like there was something in his pocket anyway. A deck of cards. But he had no pocket. A thin gown. No shirt. No pockets. His arms were bare. The deck of cards was under his skin. It didn't hurt, but there was a deck of cards under the skin of his chest. And stitches like whiskers. He shut his eyes tight. For a few moments he thought he was going to throw up. There must be some reason for this. Ed was sure that it was only time he had slipped out of and not out of the world he knew. He was still in the world. He was still alive. It wouldn't make sense that, if he were dead, they would put a deck of cards under the skin of his chest. He felt it again. His fingers tingled and shied away, but he made them go on and softly feel the thing. It was smaller than a deck of cards. It had rounded edges. It was like a little battery pack. He opened his eyes. "A pacemaker, you fool!" He smiled. "I'll be go to hell! A pacemaker."

He knew guys who had pacemakers. They walked around just like they always had with those things inside them. He saw George Bolton on the square in Half Moon. The sun was shining and George was standing in front of him. George looked a little pale, but he looked fine, really. He was skinny, but George was always skinny and Ed remembered wanting to ask George about that pacemaker thing. What was it like having that thingamajig inside of you to keep your heart beating? How could you trust a thing some guys made more than you trusted your own heart? What did it feel like? He did ask George that. "What's it feel like, George?" "Oh, you get used to feeling it. The weird thing is that you can hear it. Listen here." And George motioned for him to listen to his breast pocket. There on the street, Ed put his ear down next to George's chest and he could hear it, a clicking like the control box on an electric fence, off and on. It was pretty interesting. Ed listened, but he could hear no clicking from his own chest. He put his fingers on his neck. There it was. His pulse. They probably made these things quieter now, whenever now is. George had his put in a long time ago, maybe longer ago than he thought. No, maybe that was a valve, George's clicking. But that was too much to try to figure now. The water.

He tried again to pull the plastic off the cup. He looked around for some sharp surface to tear it against. But the corners of everything—the bars on the side of the bed, the table over the bed, the nightstand—were rounded. "So you can't slash your wrists, probably." There was nothing he could reach that was sharp. "Almost nothing." Ed rubbed the toes of one foot against the calf of the other leg. He grinned. "The fools. I could slash my wrists with my own toenails." He pushed the table to the side of the bed and slowly drew one foot up to where he could reach it. He moved the covers off, trying not to see that tube coming out of him down there. "Jesus!" He brought the plastic cup down to his foot and slashed the plastic with the horny nail of his big toe. He put his leg back down under the cover and pulled the table back and set the cup and the plastic down for a minute so he could catch his breath. Then he shakily poured himself a glass of water. The first sip he could barely taste or feel, his mouth was so dry and caked. But that second sip was the best drink of water he ever had. And by the third, he knew he was not in Illinois; it didn't taste like Illinois water.

The door opened. He hadn't noticed the door. A black woman walked in. She was packed tight inside her pale blue pants and top. Ed set the water down. She was talking loud to someone out in the hall. "He *is* moving around. I told you, Louise. I could see it on the monitor." Then she came in and leaned her big stomach up against the bars of the bed and touched his arm and smoothed his hair like this was not the first time she'd ever touched him. It felt good, that hand on his face. It felt good to know that someone was looking after him when he didn't know where he was or what was happening. Ed closed his eyes and felt some tears squeeze out. "You're OK now, honey," she said. "You're just fine. I've been watching you on TV all night and most of today and you are doing just fine."

"What's your name?" Ed asked. It came out like a croak and not as friendly as he meant it.

But she smiled anyway. "Sunny," she said.

"That's your name?"

"That's right. That's my name, not what I'm calling you." This woman had a Southern accent, but he thought maybe a lot of black people had Southern accents, no matter where they came from.

"The real question," she said, "is who are *you*?"

"Did I come in here with no wallet on me? You mean you don't know my name?" Ed got a picture of himself being hit on the back of the head and a couple of teenaged jerks taking his wallet, but he was pretty sure the picture was one from TV.

"*I* know who you are," Sunny said smiling. "I just want to know if *you* know who you are."

"I'm Ed Check from Half Moon, Illinois."

"That's right," she said proudly, as if she had more access to that information than he did. "Who is the president of the United States?"

"Reagan or somebody," Ed said.

"You don't know who?" she asked, her eyes widening.

"It don't *matter* who. They're all the same."

"Well, then, who's the vice president?" she said, laughing.

"That creep, Bush, unless I've been out cold for years."

"Mr. Check, you sure *do* know what's going on." She was holding his hand and Ed was trying to remember the last time a woman, other than Janet, had held his hand.

"Well, what year is it?"

Ed watched her face. He almost hoped she didn't notice that she was holding his hand, so she wouldn't have a reason to stop. "You're going to have to help me with this. "I *think*," he said, "it's 1988, but I really don't know how long I've been out of it. The last thing I remember, I was in my ex-wife's house in Half Moon. She was wearing an orange bathrobe and I was getting ready to ask her to marry me, or I did ask her to marry me. . . ." Ed looked toward the window. "No, I didn't ask her. I got mad about something and I left. I can see that much." He looked back at the nurse. She had a kind face and she was still holding his hand, her hand full of life and warmth. His own hands felt dry and rough, just bones and arthritis. "I'm almost afraid to ask," he said, "but where am I?"

"You're in the VA Med Center."

"Where at? In what state?"

"You're in Memphis, Tennessee."

"Any idea," he said, "*why* I'm in Memphis, Tennessee?"

"I couldn't tell you that, honey, but maybe your son can tell you. He's been here most of the time. I think he's asleep out in the waiting room. You want me to go get him?"

His son? What the hell was going on?

"Before you do, tell me what is wrong with me. Just tell me in regular words." Ed gripped her hand and was embarrassed for wanting so much for her to keep her hand there.

"What happened was you passed out the day before yesterday, probably partly because of the heat, and your son brought you in here to the emergency room. Doctor found that you had some irregularities in your heart rhythm—you've probably been having it for a while—and, with your son's permission, they put in a pacemaker. You should be fine for another thirty years, if you don't forget to get new batteries put in."

"I was pretty sure I'd be fine. I've got some business to attend to, but I'll be damned if I can remember what it is at the moment."

"Your son will help you. He's real concerned about you. I'll go get him." She let go of his hand and left the room. Ed wondered if she'd be back. And who his son could be.

A black woman had held his hand. Ed had always wondered if he was a prejudiced man and now he knew he was not. Or now he knew that *now* he was not. There wasn't enough time left to worry about who did or did not hold your hand; categories smaller than "human being" seemed not to matter, if they ever did. The sky out the window was white, the dull white that up in Illinois meant heat. It probably meant heat here, too. But this room was fine. Air-conditioned. Then at the edge of his hearing he could hear all the big background hum that was the sound of the building breathing. Who could be calling himself Ed's son? He knew he had three daughters, and he checked himself out on their names. Mary Edith. Katherine Janet. Victoria Marlene. He closed his eyes and tried to relax the tension in his jaw and upper arms. His son. He had a son-in-law. He had Jack Hawn. Maybe it was Jack. Why would it be Jack? What was going on?

The heavy door whooshed open and a woman walked in. It was Sunny. Behind her was a tall man. Then, with her hand on the man's back, she ushered him over to the bed and positioned him at the bars. Ed wished his vision wasn't so slow. He blinked a few times and then he saw it was Carl Hawn. "Carl!" he cried, and then he was again weeping; he couldn't help it. He was glad to see that he still really was connected to Half Moon. Ed was bawling with his forearm over his eyes, and the woman was saying, "Sometimes the anesthetic does this," but Ed knew it was relief and other things he didn't remember. Carl put his arm awkwardly around Ed's back. On Carl's shirt Ed could smell old cigarettes and Carl himself and an unfamiliar smell that was this city. Memphis, Tennessee. That odd business in the light that he saw this morning must be the Mississippi River. The sky over water. Ed sniffed and wiped his eyes on the bedspread. He sat up and Carl drew his arm away. "Can you reach me a Kleenex over there, Carly Boy?"

Carl gave him a handful of tissues and Ed blew his nose. "What time is it?"

"A little after four o'clock." Carl pulled a chair over beside the bed.

Ed raised his bed up so he could see Carl better. "What day is it?"

"It's Friday."

"And?"

"It's August 19."

"One more."

"1988," added Carl, grinning.

"I was just checking," Ed said.

"On who?" Carl asked.

Ed and Carl were silent as they watched Sunny fussing around the room. She took Ed's blood pressure and then straightened the covers around him. She unwrapped the bandage over the IV going in his arm and tapped a few times on the needle. Carl looked away, but she hadn't hurt him. Then she checked the bag of fluid going in and emptied the one coming out into a measuring cup and carried it into the bathroom. Carl got up and went to the window and sat down on the wide sill. Ed watched Sunny in the bathroom. She wrote some numbers down on a sheet on the door and then dumped his piss into the toilet. When she turned to come out, she saw him watching and said, "We're measuring your urine."

"You are."

She nodded. "Mr. Check—"

"Call me Ed."

She was beside the bed holding his hand again. "Ed, you're on solid food now so dinner will be in pretty quick." Ed watched her give Carl the once-over. He saw her see his jeans with holes in them, his faded and frayed shirt, the worn shoes. He saw her notice—and then he did too—how skinny Carl was and that he cut his own ragged hair. At home Carl looked fine, but in this strange place he looked like a man who was not taken care of and it was true. His face seemed like one you shouldn't take out in public, since it was not one used to defending itself from the eyes of strangers. There was none of the artificial or planned stuff in it that kept strangers' eyes off your insides. He realized he was squeezing Sunny's hand and he loosened his grip.

"Ed," she was telling him, "most of the time when they bring up the trays, they get the count wrong and there's too many. Tell your son to stick around; there'll probably be a dinner for him. Let's hope it's not a really weird one—'soft diet' or 'low sodium.'"

"When are they going to let me out of here?" he asked Sunny.

"I heard the doctor mention something about Monday, but he'll be in to talk to you about that. And later somebody will be in to help you take a walk down the hall." Then she left, shutting the door behind her.

Ed felt a strange lack of curiosity about what had brought him to Memphis. He could wait to find that out. But he wanted to know what this place was like. "Carl, what do you see from that window?"

"Well," Carl said, turning to look out, "downtown Memphis, which from here looks like a big city. But mainly what I see is the Mississippi River. We are pretty high up—on the seventh floor—so I can see a lot of the river in both directions. There's two bridges, one of them kind of looping. From here, the superstructure on that one looks like a flying bird, a crow or the way a kid would draw a crow. That might be the bridge we came over on the interstate, but I'm not sure. There's a couple barges on the river—one going up river and one going down. The one going down will pass by Vicksburg, I bet," and Carl turned around to look at Ed.

Then Ed remembered it all. They were on their way to Vicksburg to get Vickie. He remembered Vickie's postcard, and he asked Carl for it.

"I got both of them right here," Carl said, and from his shirt pocket he took the house one and the one with the view of the river and he handed them to Ed. The big old house. Her girlish writing. The address of the house. "Carl, I've got to call her."

"We are five hours or so north of Vicksburg," Carl said. "I've asked around."

"Do you think I could call her from this phone?"

"No long-distance calls," Carl said.

"You checked into that too?"

"I did." Carl got up out of the chair he had just sat down in. He paced over to the window and looked out again. "Those barges move pretty fast," he said. "Downstream, anyway." He sat back down in the chair.

"What is it, Carl?" Ed asked, but he didn't mean to hurry him.

"Well, before you were in surgery, I made some calls. I called Janet and talked to her several times. She knows what happened and that you're going to be OK now, and she knows what we were on our way to do, but we thought she shouldn't say anything to anyone in town about it just yet. She's worried, but she talked to the doctor and he didn't think it was necessary for her to come down here. You'll be home in a few days." Carl stopped and took a breath and crossed his arms over his chest, putting his hands in his armpits.

"Has she heard from Jack yet?" Ed thought that maybe whatever Carl wasn't telling him had to do with Jack and Janet.

"No," he said. "Nobody has." He took a deep breath. "Yesterday I called Vickie," he said. "I figured you'd want me to. You were in a hurry."

"You talked to her?"

"I did."

"Is she OK?"

"She is. She's fine."

"Is Marlene with her?"

"No. Vickie's staying with some women who run a bed-and-breakfast place and she's helping them out. It sounds like they are taking good care of her, too."

"My god," Ed said. "My god. You talked to Vickie."

"She wants to see her dad." Carl waited while Ed just stared at him. "She's quite a young lady, Ed."

"How does she sound?"

"Well, she sounds like someone who knows her own mind, someone who can look out for herself. She sounds older than twenty, to me. She has a pretty voice with a little bit of a Southern accent."

Ed smiled. It was too much to take in. "I'm goddamned glad I've got this pacer, but I think it slows down my brain too."

"Are you OK, Ed?" Carl came over to the bed and leaned on the bed rails. "Do you want me to leave you alone for a bit?"

Ed heard him, but he was back on "pretty voice" and "Marlene wasn't with her," trying to take in those two things at once.

Carl said, "Ed, I'm going to go out and come back around seven. I'm going to let you think about this and then I'll be back."

Ed hauled himself on the rope of time to the here and now. "Carl, where are you staying?"

"Well, that's kind of interesting. I met this couple in a bar, right down the street. Real nice people. From here in Memphis. We got to talking and I told them what was going on, and pretty soon they were asking me to stay at their place so I didn't have to sleep in the truck. Real nice people. Don and Linda Monroe. They want to come see you when you feel up to it."

"I feel up to it now."

"You rest now. Maybe I'll bring them back tonight."

"What I'd really like to do is leave this minute to go get Vickie."

"We'll talk about that. Right now she's fine where she is. She's really OK, Ed. You rest." For a moment Carl put his hand over Ed's hand. Then he left.

Ed took the house postcard in his hand and brought it to his face, where he could see the picture on the front. The house was above the level of the street and there were wide brick steps going up to the front porch of the house. He counted them. Fifteen steps. There was a white wooden railing beside the steps and when you got to the top you would stand in front of a tall white double door. Ed could see himself climbing those steps. He could feel the brick under his feet. He counted his steps to the top. He felt the cool as he came out of the hot sun into the shade of the porch and when he reached out his hand he felt the chalky paint on the tall white pillar. There were four pillars. He stood a moment at the top of the step and turned and looked at what he could see from there. He brought the other postcard to his face. There was the river. He could see miles of it from the porch. The dark green forests below the bluffs. Then the wide brown river curving out of sight both north and south, the currents making the surface rich and burnished, smooth and rough. Beyond that the tan shore and flat forested land as far as his eye could see. And the two bridges close together — a black one and a silver one. All of this, silent in the heat of a Mississippi afternoon. Next Monday afternoon. He turned back to the house. The four long, narrow windows were curtained in lace. Beside the door was a bell and when he rang it he heard its chimes deep in the house. A nice woman came to the door. She had her hair in braids on top of her head the way Edith used to wear her hair. She had been waiting for him and she took him into a fancy sitting room and sat him down where he could face the door that Vickie would come through. Then he heard her light step on the stair, coming down fast. And then the door opened and his youngest girl rushed into his arms. After a long time of holding her, he made her go sit on the couch so he could look at her. Ed put the postcards down and closed his eyes.

She was as small as he was. She had his hands and feet. But her hair was medium brown like her mother's— thick and wavy and down to her shoulders. She looked like Marlene—the same wide mouth and dark eyebrows and lashes. The same light brown eyes in which you could see how smart she was and how strong. The same cheekbones and the same nose that was ridiculously small. She had on a green skirt and white blouse. She was slim and she couldn't sit still. And she had her mother's laugh. For a long time Ed watched her sitting on the couch in that room, smiling at him.

"Dinner, Ed!" A woman was bringing him a tray. She set it down on the table across the bed and took off the plastic covers. Ed smelled steamed food. "You need any help?" she asked, standing beside the door.

"You might bring me my teeth," Ed said, wondering what this stuff was. Oh good, it was labeled. According to the narrow sheet that came with it, this was baked chicken, low-fat gravy, rice, green beans, bread and margarine, and Jell-O. He'd take their word for it.

She brought him his teeth in a little plastic container and he put them in. When he started to eat, it all tasted wonderful. He couldn't remember when food had tasted so good to him.

The woman who'd brought him his dinner left the

door open so while he ate he saw now and then men wearing bathrobes shuffling past the door. Sometimes he saw women, but the women all were dressed—in regular clothes or the pale blue getups the nurses wore. There was a fair amount of talk out in the hall, but he couldn't catch the words. He liked the way they talked here; it reminded him of the time when he was a young man and had gone to New Orleans with Kenny. It was all interesting—the way things tasted, the sound of the voices in the hallway, the way the men walked.

When another woman came in to pick up his tray, he asked her if she could look for his glasses. She found them in the nightstand beside the bed and handed them to him, but she was either busy or that wasn't her job, because she was not pleased to do it. When he put his glasses on, the peeved look on her face came into focus.

He waited with his glasses on and his teeth in, and while he waited he tried to see more out the window, but it was still only sky that he could see. Now the sun was setting, so the sky was pale yellow at the top and there was some green too, but mostly it was rose and orange. All of this with the river, too, would be something to see.

Later he did see the tail end of the sunset when another woman came to take him for a walk. It was a pretty big deal considering all the lines and equipment he was hooked up to that had to go along with him. But he held onto the pole on wheels that she'd hung his IV bag on, and with the pole on one side and her on the other, he walked over to the window where she let him stand for a moment and then she steered him out into the hall where there were a bunch of other old men and some not-so-old men walking too. Some had poles and women like he did. Some just had poles. And some just had women. Ed grinned at the odd parade and at his embarrassing weakness. But the woman told him over and over that he was doing just fine.

When she had him situated back in his room and someone fixed it so he was no longer peeing into a tube, he did feel fine. Marlene wasn't with Vickie, but he felt fine. He would go up those fifteen steps in a few days — slowly, for sure — and he would see his daughter and take her home to Half Moon.

He sat and rested and dozed with his hands across his stomach and he remembered a thing or two of the trip down here with Carl.

They had been on the interstate in Carl's truck. Ed noticed brown things that were shaped like leaves but didn't move like leaves. They kept swirling up beside the truck and sometimes onto the windshield. He said to Carl, "Those brown, leafy things we keep seeing, those would be . . . ?"

"Right," said Carl. "Monarchs."

"Monarchs," Ed had said. "On their way to Mexico. And on our way to Vicksburg, we knock 'em off."

"It's a shame, isn't it?" Carl said. "All that way from up north to get hit by a pickup truck on I-55."

"A lot of dead animals on the road, too, if I'm not mistaken. All kinds."

He remembered that, and he remembered the pleasure they both took in those hours of driving fairly fast in a truck across flat land. He remembered watching groves of trees — always blue with haze and distance — rise up and run beside the truck and recede behind him under the curve of the earth. He remembered the battering of the hot air from the open windows, and the different smells the air took on as they neared the river or as the land was sandy or red clay. He remembered the smell of pesticide and natural gas and, around St. Louis, a pleasant city smell of exhaust fumes and people living on low, damp land.

He remembered something else that must have been in Memphis. It was on a city street lined with dusty and run-down brick buildings. The sun was low and at their backs—it felt like the sun was just across the river—and there didn't seem to be any trees in Memphis. People were not on the street either, just a few cars and them and the sun. He had never felt heat like that. It was so bad he could barely see through it. You couldn't talk in it. They were stopped for a long time at a red light, where they could feel the heat coming up at them off the street and the sidewalks. A young man came out of his house carrying his little baby. He carried it like this was not something he did very often, but it was something he didn't mind doing. He had the baby facing away from him, the yellow pajamas and bobbing peach-colored head against the man's red shirt. He was walking west toward the lowering sun, which shone in the baby's eyes, but the man didn't notice. The baby blinked and, as much as it could, put its fists toward its eyes.

Ed woke up when Carl came back and the room was full of the last red light of that day. While he was asleep, someone must have taken out the IV, because now he was not hooked up to anything and he could get out of bed if he wanted.

"Get me that robe over there, Carl, so my ass doesn't hang out." And Carl helped him over to the window where they stood and now Ed could see that that bridge did look like a crow or maybe a gull, as he said to Carl. And you could see it clearly because it was outlined in yellow lights that were reflected in the river.

Carl was excited about something. Ed had seen that

when he first walked in. He'd put on his other, better, shirt and it looked like he'd gotten a haircut.

Ed sat down on the chair by the window and Carl sat on the bed. It looked to Ed like some new idea was propping him up.

"Carl," Ed said. "I want to ask you a personal question."

Carl looked a little nervous. "What?"

"Did you get your hair cut since this afternoon?"

Carl grinned. "Don and Linda—that couple I was telling you about? Well, Linda is a beautician and she offered to cut it. Right there in the kitchen. She cuts Don's hair too."

"It looks good. You ought to do that more often."

"Yeah, I know. I ought to do a lot of stuff more often, and a lot of stuff less often."

"Like what?"

"I ought to drink less often. And go hear music like we did last night. A live band in a bar." Carl's eyes were lit up in a way Ed hadn't seen them in years. "Ed," he said, his arms shaking from excitement, "I'm going to stop drinking. I'm going to try. There's too many people out there. Too much I'm missing. I'm going to try."

Ed thought of all the times he had heard that from Marlene. He wished he could believe him.

"But listen, Ed, here's the neat thing. Remember I said we were about five hours away from Vicksburg? Well, Don and Linda want to drive me down there tomorrow and we'll pick up Vickie and her stuff and then drive back here on Sunday. Then she can go back to Half Moon with us Monday or Tuesday. These people have a van."

Ed could see Vickie on Sunday. She could walk into this room on Sunday afternoon or evening. She would walk into this hospital room and see her old man after all these years in a nightgown and bathrobe. What about those fifteen steps and the porch and the nice living room? He would have to cut that picture loose. He wanted to be the one to go get Vickie and bring her back safe and sound.

"These people," he said to Carl, "Linda and Don? You've only known them a short time. Are they . . . reliable?"

"Ed," Carl said, "would I go with them to get Vickie if I wasn't sure?"

"No, you wouldn't." He had trusted one daughter to Jack; he had to trust this daughter to Carl.

"They want to meet you in the morning. They want us to stop by on our way."

"Have you talked to Vickie and the women she is working for about this?"

"I called and made all the arrangements. I just have to call back and let her know if it's all right with you."

Ed cut loose his picture and in its place he saw one of Carl going up those steps for Vickie. Ed nodded and Carl left, and Ed lay back in the bed. Pictures of Marlene were drifting away too.

14

When Vickie woke between cool ironed sheets in the little bed, she could hear the house below her—the creaking of the floors even though no one else was up and the quiet sounds of the street filtered all the way through the big rooms to the top and back of the house where she lay. And through the open window there came the beginning sounds of the birds below and the fresh smell of the summer morning. But this was the last time she would wake here; this was the morning she was to leave Mrs. Phillipa Merton's house. No.

She sat up in bed, her legs scissoring in the sheets to get all the coolness and the rich smooth feel of the cloth she now knew was linen. Last night she had secretly borrowed these sheets from the closet in the second-floor hallway. The creamy top sheet hung to the floor on either side of her narrow bed, and the heavy lace edging felt like jewelry in her hands, even in her sleep.

This morning she was stronger than she had ever been in her life—her arms and legs were lengths of steel—but this strength, which made moving effortless around the hard and growing center of her, came not from sleep and the sheets and all the good food, but from rage. Rage at her mother, at Bo, at all the ignorant strangers, at the women downstairs, at her stupid past and the hard, inescapable future that grew inside of her, which she had to carry everywhere. She wanted *this* for her future, this house, the rose and silvery room just below her, the white kitchen, the wide and curving stairway, the quiet of the big rooms downstairs, the cupboards full of linens and dishes, and those little red glasses that seemed carved out of rubies.

But today some people were coming to take her to a little farm town up in Illinois. She couldn't even take her car, they all said, because it wasn't her car, it was Bo's car. Mavis said her brother would "take care of it." And they weren't taking her to the farm she remembered. And it wasn't her father who was coming for her, but her father's neighbor, a man she didn't know, a farmer who was the brother of the man who married her half sister. The people with him were a hairdresser and a man who sang in a band.

She wasn't ready to go. She didn't want to go. The women had helped her pack, had given her clothes for her baby, but Vickie couldn't remember how to get ready to leave. Now her father was an old man in a hospital in Memphis and he might not even live, and then what would happen to her? Her mother had said that her father was a good man, but that she felt she could "poke her finger right through him." How could you depend on a person like that?

Mrs. Phillipa Merton had arranged this whole thing; she just jumped at the chance to get rid of Vickie, though Vickie had dusted for her for almost two months and had not broken a thing, not one cup or saucer. And Vickie had helped Mavis every day in the kitchen. Mavis said she had a light touch with biscuits, with all the baking; both of them said she was a natural in the kitchen. And she was. She made spoon bread and pilau and oyster fritters and chicken croquettes, and a tray of her little cut sandwiches was as pretty as if she had been born in this house. But now she had to leave. "You should be with your family," they both said, though what Phillipa really meant was, "You should get out of my house before your baby and your being single embarrass me." Vickie didn't know what Mavis really meant, but at least Mavis had cried when she said it. Phillipa Merton's eyes could not cry, Vickie was sure of that; they could glitter, though, in a way that even she would not argue with.

The sheets were warm all over now from her legs and the heat at the center of her, so she was out of bed and standing at the window, looking down at the quiet garden. She was too big for this tiny little bedroom and this tiny bed. She wanted to fly at all of them, all the people, tear them apart with screams and her hands. But this baby left her little room for breathing or screaming. She should be down in the pink room below in a bed with curtains around it and a white canopy over it. Instead she was squeezed high up in this tiny room in this other woman's house and why couldn't it be her house? She had as much right to all this as anyone. Why did it have to belong to the one woman who wanted her out of the house now? Why couldn't it at least belong to Mavis? The garden below and the brick walls and the shiny-leaved bushes—why weren't they hers? Vickie felt she could easily tear up the bricks with her bare hands and shred the bushes.

The people who were coming for her would be here at lunchtime. She was supposed to help Mavis make a lunch for them. Mrs. Phillipa Merton had said, "Anyone, no matter who they are, if they are connected with our Vickie"—she now knew Vickie's real name—"will be treated with respect and hospitality in my home." Phillipa had been seated at the little telephone table in the back hall. She had just hung up the phone after talking to Vickie's father's friend; his name was Carl Hawn. A very plain name. Phillipa had just said to this stranger that Vickie was "expecting a little baby in October, though she is just a child herself. Were you aware of those circumstances?" Vickie didn't know what the man said, but she could tell that Phillipa was surprised. She said, "You are a tolerant and accepting man. I hope Vickie's father is of the same mind." The man apparently said he was because Mrs. Phillipa Merton said, "That's good, that's good," though you could tell she did not quite know what to think. Mrs. Merton's voice was most sweet when she was most disgusted, so Vickie could tell that she did not think that Vickie's "people" were up to her own standards. They were not the sort of people she would let sleep in her four big rooms—the rose one, the blue one, the green one, the yellow one. Vickie was glad that she had, once or twice a week if there were no guests in the house, sneaked down the back stairs after the others were asleep and slipped into the bed in the rose and silver room, slipped between the pale pink sheets and slept there. Or rather, slipped into the pale pink sheets and lay there daydreaming of herself as the owner of this house.

Vickie stood at the window of the house in Vicksburg in one of Phillipa's old cotton nightgowns. There was still no one awake in the house below her. She stood leaning against the windowsill until her baby gave a kick that made her jump. "Cripes, Cornelia!" She still called her baby Cornelia when she thought it was a girl, and when she thought it was a boy she called it Edward Wilton.

The birds below her were starting up for real now. She had better hurry. Up to that moment she hadn't known that she was going to take the book with the picture of Wilton. And the little red glasses.

Without putting on her clothes or the slippers Mavis gave her or the bathrobe they called a dressing gown, Vickie went down the back stairs to the second floor and, soundless on the wool rugs, slipped into Mrs. Merton's parlor at the front of the house. She went right to the book in the bookcase, took it out without a sound, and moved the books together to cover the empty space. Then she went back upstairs to her bedroom and opened one of the two boxes that Mavis and Mrs. Merton had packed for her yesterday afternoon. She took out the carefully folded maternity dresses and the nice underwear and on the bottom of the box she put the book with the pictures of Wilton and then she carefully put everything back. She opened the other box to look again at the tiny shirts and sleepers that the two women had given to Vickie. It was only when she looked at these little clothes that the baby seemed real to her. She couldn't look for long, but she liked the perfect little shirts and most of these things were not even used. Mavis and Phillipa had bought these things for her baby. But Phillipa, at least, had given her these things because she felt bad at sending her off, at sending her out of this house when Vickie wanted to stay here and later stand on the porch holding her baby and nod and wave to the women who walked by on the sidewalk below.

And now some stranger had found her and was taking her up to Memphis where she would see her father this same day and then they would go up north to Illinois and she would live in the old Half Moon Hotel which she remembered as practically falling down.

Still in her nightgown, Vickie stood at the top of the stairs and listened. No sound came yet from Mavis's room at the end of the third-floor hallway, and no sound came from downstairs. It was early. No water had rattled the pipes yet this morning. Again she ran downstairs, this time the back stairs, cool and slick under her bare feet; she was fast and surefooted; she felt as if she could fly, one hand on the banister, the other holding her belly.

But she was strong; her arms and legs were strong. What could she do to use this strength? What was it for? As she ran down the stairs she wondered if she would always feel this way, that she was full of strength and possibilities but also too full of anger and baby and the stupid past to do anything, to be anyone.

The dining-room walls were a buttery yellow that always made Vickie hungry. When she had a dining room she would paint the walls yellow, too, so that people would feel there that the sun was shining and they were hungry but there was plenty to eat. She stood in front of a dish cupboard that Mrs. Phillipa Merton had called Federal. That was a style of furniture that Vickie knew she didn't like. There were too many curves and eagles and the dark wood depressed her. There were four glass doors in the top of this Federal dish cupboard, and two doors below that, and four drawers in the middle. The gold eagle which reminded Vickie of the man with the scissors was way over her head perched in the center of the cupboard almost at the ceiling. Behind one of the glass doors there were three shelves of red glasses, which, when the sun was just right, looked like a fire inside the cupboard. Some of the glasses were wine glasses, and some were water glasses—goblets, Mrs. Phillipa Merton called them, but Vickie hated that word. It had an ugly sound and these were so beautiful, these red glasses, especially the twelve tiny ones, which were not for children but they looked like they could be. The others were stemware, but these were tiny straight-sided glasses. There were twelve of them. Vickie took six.

Upstairs, when she had packed the glasses at the bottom of one of the boxes and when she had caught her breath, Vickie took the linen sheets off the bed and folded them the way they had been folded in the linen closet. Then she took the muslin sheets that had been on the bed and put them in the upstairs hamper. After that she quickly bathed for the last time in the big tub and she washed her hair and left it to wave naturally. She put on the dark green leaf-printed maternity dress that Mrs. Phillipa Merton was letting her take with her and packed up her toothbrush and toothpaste and shampoo and she was ready to go. As she put the linen sheets back in the linen closet, she began to think of the day ahead. At lunchtime she would meet these people who were coming for her. At the end of the day she would see her father.

Down in the kitchen she looked at the round clock hanging high up on the wall. No wonder it was so quiet. It was barely six. Vickie unlatched the heavy back door and opened it, and then she pushed open the screen door and stepped out into the yard, which was still shadowy and damp and smelled like grass and other things she wished she could name. The magnolia leaves, thick like wallets, made her feel that everything she wanted was out of her reach.

Back in the kitchen she stood in the middle and turned slowly around so she could memorize it. She wanted to remember the particular way the dim light came through the magnolia and then warmed up when it came into the white, no, cream-colored, tiled room. She wanted to remember the glass and wood doors over the counters and all the pots and pans and dishes you could ever want or need. The oven door that screeched. The big white sink where she sometimes washed Mrs. Phillipa Merton's thin hair if Erma in the beauty parlor's mother was sick. The wood table where she chopped things up for Mavis and where she read stacks of recipe books with her after breakfast before they started in on a tea or a luncheon because Mrs. Phillipa Merton rented her parlor for "affairs" and Mavis made the food.

Mavis, Phillipa had said, was the best cook in Vicksburg and many of the ladies wanted Mavis, but Mavis
was loyal, she said, and loved her work. Mavis may be
loyal, but she could see through Phillipa and she hated to
cook. Vickie knew because Mavis had told her she was
sick of cooking. She wanted to do something else. She
wanted to go to Hawaii. They weren't so prejudiced there,
she'd read, and you could just eat salads. Still, when
Vickie and Mavis had sat down after breakfast and pored
over old cookbooks and a few new ones, it was hard
to tell that Mavis hated to cook. She loved to answer
Vickie's questions about what's the difference between
beaten and rolled biscuits and what the heck is spoon
bread and what is guinea squash, which she read a
recipe for in one of the old books. It turned out that's
what some people used to call eggplant — guinea squash.

Then Vickie sat down fast at the big table and she put
her head down on her arms because she was crying.
Fuck. She didn't want to leave. How could she leave? She
knew what was what around here, the names of things
and the connections between people and between the
present and the past, and now she had to leave. It was
like it had always been with her mother. Just when you
begin to let yourself settle down, she ripped you up and
moved you on. How could she never be in this house
again when she knew so much: what Mavis's dresses always smelled like, and the way she always got her but-
tons caught on the handle of the dishwasher, all about
her sons and her daughters-in-law, and about Mavis's
grandmother and the way she made pound cake and the
way she made roast pork and the way she pickled okra —
when two months ago she didn't even know what okra
was. Vickie sniffed and leaned down and wiped her nose
on the inside of the hem of her skirt and then she looked
up again at that dim light coming in through the magno-

lia tree. "This is the last time," she said. "The next place I wind up, if it's halfway decent, I'm staying there. I will find a way to tie myself tight to that place." And then she straightened her skirt as Phillipa would and took down from the shelf one of the cookbooks, because she'd be damned if she'd make a bad lunch for these people who were coming to get her. She had to remember that everything she did was for the two of them now—her and Cornelia or her and Edward Wilton. Maybe three, if you counted her father.

She started some coffee as Mavis had taught her and got down the breakfast cups and plates, the napkins in their rings, and the silverware. She got the bread out and the eggs and the bacon. While she drank her coffee, only one cup a day because of the baby, she would look through the cookbooks and figure out what they would cook to impress these people.

Yesterday Phillipa had gotten three small chickens and she said that Vickie and Mavis could make whatever they wanted with the chickens and they could use anything in the pantry except the cans of crabmeat. So. Vickie had three cookbooks—*Recipes from Southern Kitchens, Charleston Receipts,* and a splattered one with the cover gone that was Mavis's favorite. "Receipts" was an old-fashioned word for recipe, she had learned from Mavis. Mavis thought *Charleston Receipts* was Vickie's favorite cookbook because she thought Vickie liked anything old-fashioned, which was true since she had been here, but the real reason that Vickie liked this cookbook was because the recipes came from actual women in Charleston in 1950, and she never got tired of reading their names.

Each woman had two names. After the recipe for Asparagus Mousseline it said Mrs. James Hagood (Antoinette Camp). After Vegetable Salad, Mrs. Simons Vander Horst Waring (Louisa Johnson); Mallow Mint Sauce, Mrs. M.L.

McCrae (Ena Mae Black); Mint Parfait, Mrs. Arthur J. Stoney (Anne Montague); Sweet Potato Pie, Mrs. Thomas Waring, Jr. (Clelia Mathewes).

How could these women with two names be just one woman? Vickie knew that if you grew up as Clelia Mathewes and then became Mrs. Thomas Waring, Jr., you would have to change. You would have to become someone else. You would have to become *for* someone else. Vickie liked their girl names and saw the unmarried Charleston women as free and flighty and noisy as birds. Their married names quieted them and held them down to the place and to houses and to families. She wanted both for herself—a flighty, pretty girl name and a serious woman name that held her to a place. But she had neither. Vickie Check was a stupid girl name. And though she was carrying a baby, which held her down, it didn't hold her to one place or family. She never thought of Bo as having anything to do with this baby. She would never see Bo again and now she knew that Bo was the sort of person that Phillipa Merton called trash.

By the time Mavis came downstairs, the day was already very hot and Vickie could tell from one look at the set of Mavis's mouth and the squint and glitter of her eyes that this was "one of her days." Phillipa had long ago warned Vickie about Mavis's "days," and she was right. There were days when Mavis would not say word one and from the look on her face you could be just as glad she was keeping whatever she was thinking to herself. Vickie's mother had had "days" too, but hers all had to do with one of three things—a man, the curse, or a hangover. Vickie had no idea what Mavis's days were about and she didn't think Mrs. Phillipa Merton did either, because Phillipa would just shrug her shoulders and sigh when she saw that look and she would adjust as you would to bad weather.

Mavis sat down heavily at the table with her cup of black coffee, and it was as if Vickie didn't even exist.

Vickie turned away from her, put two pieces of bread in the toaster, and made her voice sound like she hadn't noticed Mavis's face. "What do you think about chicken croquettes for lunch today? For when those people are here?" Mavis didn't answer.

Vickie went to the refrigerator for butter. Mavis drank her coffee, leafing through the open cookbook in front of her.

Vickie made herself busy at the stove with breaking eggs and buttering toast. She kept her back to Mavis. The only thing she could do when her mother was like this was pretend that such a mood did not exist.

Mavis still didn't say anything. Vickie ate her eggs and toast standing on the back step dreaming of the day when, in a place of her own, she would not have to deal with the craziness of other people.

She went back in the kitchen and stood at the sink, rinsing her plate. Mavis said, "It's too goddamned hot for chicken croquettes. Fix chicken salad."

Vickie didn't see how she could boil and bone, then cool, three chickens before twelve o'clock, but by the time Mrs. Merton came down for breakfast an hour later, the air in the kitchen was hot with the smell of boiling chicken, as well as poisonous from Mavis and Vickie's moods. Mrs. Merton walked around the kitchen in her frilly bathrobe eating a triangle of toast and chattering about this and that until she couldn't stand it anymore. "*I'm* taking my coffee *upstairs*. Y'all are no *fun* this morning."

The morning passed slowly. Mavis went to her room and stayed there. Vickie was alone in the kitchen, moving slowly in the heat that made nothing matter. She made the chicken salad, faintly enjoying the quiet of the kitchen, the slow and repetitious motions of the knife in her hand on chicken and pickles and celery. She watched her hands hull strawberries, peel eggs, peel cucumbers. Her hands seemed a long way away as she mashed warm egg yolks with mayonnaise and curry, filled the slippery whites with yellow. She circled again and again the dining-room table, setting out place mats and napkins, plates and glasses, knives and forks and spoons. The heat and the circling and the baby made her feel she was not even human, but she didn't care. Sweat darkened her dress; sweat ran down her thighs; on her upper lip the sweat stung and she didn't even lick it off.

When the doorbell rang at 12:30, it rang in a silent dream house. She opened the door and let the three people in without even looking at them. She sat them in the front parlor and went for iced tea. She brought the tray of iced tea and passed it around. The woman was talking, but Vickie could barely hear her; it didn't seem to matter. The man who sat beside the woman talked too. They talked and laughed and Vickie heard herself talk. They were talking about the heat, about driving, about sticking to the upholstery of the car, about burning their hands on the steering wheel, about heat stroke, about people all over the South dropping dead from the heat.

The tall man didn't talk, and the more he didn't talk, the more Vickie looked at him through the thick air. She licked her sweaty lip and held the dripping glass and looked at the man who looked at her.

His face was thin and somewhat sharp. The other people's faces were just regular faces, but this man's face was different enough that it made Vickie want to figure out what it was like. In the heat it was the only thing that seemed to matter. The wide cheekbones and somewhat slanting eyes made her think *cat, Eskimo,* but those words weren't right; his hair was between brown and blond and even from this distance and through this heat, she could see that his eyes were blue. He stared at her, but she could see that he wasn't making any judgments, he was forming questions in his mind—he was curious—and Vickie watched herself decide that this was a man who might listen to what she would have to say and one who might look beyond her stories of herself. She saw his eyes which asked questions and his upper lip which was pushed up a little by his lower lip as if both could be hurt and she saw the old clothes that didn't matter to him one way or another, the new haircut which made her feel older than him, though he was probably twice her age. There was something about the amount of wear and tear that showed on his face that made her think of her mother and her mother's boyfriends. But it didn't matter. This man's name was Carl Hawn. The name was plain, but it was plain the same way Wilton was plain.

She didn't eat much lunch, but Carl Hawn ate a lot of chicken salad and curried eggs and so did the man and the woman who talked and talked. Mrs. Phillipa Merton talked too and there was the cheerful sound of spoons stirring sugar in the tea and forks on plates. Vickie watched Mrs. Phillipa Merton talk and she watched the place where the six red glasses had been. Only now and then did she look at the face of Carl Hawn; she would save that for later. He didn't look right in this house anyway.

Before they left, Mavis came down so that both the black woman and the white woman hugged Vickie in the hall and she laughed to herself because she was just as sweaty leaving here as she had been when they took her in. But she and the baby were bigger, much bigger. Out on the porch, the heat came down on her like more weight and she swayed a moment and reached out for the railing. Carl Hawn had put her two boxes in the back of the car and then Mavis and Mrs. Phillipa Merton hugged her and put envelopes in her hand and then, with her hand on the hot railing, she slowly went down to the street while Carl Hawn came up to her and helped her down and into the car. Vickie had never felt so far away from the rest of the people in the world, so bound by her own skin, so separate, so distinct and indifferent. This was what her strong arms and legs were for—to carry herself and her baby forward whether or not she wanted to go.

On the drive to Memphis, Vickie sat in the backseat of the beat-up old van with Carl Hawn. The heat made things simple. The man and the woman in the front seat talked and the woman turned around and smiled at Vickie and reached around and patted her on the knee, but Vickie didn't have much to say. She was so unbearably sleepy that at first she slept sitting up, and then the woman bunched up a jacket and she rested her head back on that. Then, when they were stopped for gas and for Cokes, she felt their arms push her down onto the seat and she lay there with the top of her head touching the man Carl Hawn's leg. She sat up to drink water now and then, and to see where they were, but each time she did she saw a little tract house or an apartment building or a farmhouse that she wanted to live in so much that it hurt to tear her eyes away from it and move on.

It was the man next to her who made her feel this way—that she could live anywhere. The man and the heat and the baby. She woke up once and the sun was setting over the Mississippi River—the sky was red and purple and green, almost frightening—and she spoke to herself and asked herself if she were dreaming this peacefulness and this man. She hoped it was a case of her body knowing something that she would come to know later in her mind. She looked at the sunset and saw all its colors on

Carl Hawn's face and saw him look at her and she felt herself smile. And she slept again.

In the hospital elevator going up to see her father, all three of them tried to convince her that, while she was here, she should see a doctor, but, no, she said, she was fine now, it had been the heat and the excitement of leaving that made her so drowsy and she was fine now. She told them that Dr. Sand in Vicksburg said she was healthy and strong and the baby was fine and she should have no problems. All four of them were breathless and disheveled from the wind that had come up suddenly and the fat drops of rain that had hit them like bugs when they ran from the parking lot. In the parking lot, Carl Hawn had taken her hand as they ran, and now, in the elevator, he still held it in his big hand which Vickie noticed was hard from work and not sweaty.

When the elevator opened on the floor where her father was, the man and the woman—Vickie had not bothered to remember their names—said they would wait in the lounge at the end of the hall and they headed off in the other direction. Carl Hawn said, "This way," and took her by the elbow. They passed four old men in four rooms and the fifth room Carl went in.

Vickie wanted to slow everything down; it all seemed to be happening so fast. Too late she realized she hadn't combed her hair after they came in out of the wind, and it was probably sticking up funny all over her head.

A small, old man dressed in dark green pants and a white shirt stood at the window looking out at the sky which was now dark blue and gray and purple. He didn't hear them come into the room. Vickie stood at the foot of the bed and held on to it with one hand; she smoothed her hair with the other. Her heart was beating so hard and fast she thought she might faint. Was this really happening? Was she really in the same room, after all these years, with her father? The man was very old. Maybe this wasn't her father.

Carl Hawn went up to the man and touched him on the elbow and the man turned around, smiling at Carl, keeping his eyes on Carl and keeping his smile going as if he were afraid too that this might not be happening, as if he were afraid of what he might or might not see.

The man slowly turned toward her, smiling at Carl, and Carl said, "Ed, Vickie's here."

Vickie just stood there and the man with a funny and kind and smiling face let his eyes light on her and then she began to feel tears welling up in her, nameless feelings in her chest.

"Vickie," he said.

He was looking at her face. He came up to her and put his hands on her cheeks while she hung onto the bed with both hands and the tears ran down. Then he put his hands on her head and smoothed her hair. "Just like your mother's hair," he said. Vickie was sobbing.

Her father laughed, a low and gentle chuckle. He put one arm around her shoulder and pulled her gently away from the bed that she clung to, and pulled her over to the lamp light by the window. He held both her hands and looked at her. He spoke to her and his voice was just as she remembered it, though everything else was different. "I see you brought a very nice surprise." He was looking at her big belly, but he was still smiling.

Vickie had forgotten to get ready for this; she'd forgotten to think about how she would explain. She sniffed and wiped her eyes and said, "I'm sure this is a big surprise to you; it was to me, too."

"My grandchild," he said. "I get to be a granddad." There wasn't anything in his voice that she could figure was regret or judgment. "When is he due? When do we get to see him or her?"

"October," she said. "The middle of October."

"Are you healthy?" he asked. "Is the baby?"

Vickie nodded.

He lifted her two hands and he held them close to his face. He studied her hands, front and back. Vickie realized then that her hands were swollen with the heat and she tried to pull them back. He held them tighter and she looked and saw that her hands were shaped just like his— short, round fingers and stubby fingernails and small, square palms.

"I'm so glad to see you," she said, wishing she could think of something prettier to say, something that sounded like what she felt. "I'm glad to be with you again."

"Oh, me too, honey." And then he held her tight. "We've got a lot of catching up to do, haven't we?"

While he held her, Vickie saw that the sky was dark now, the lights had come on in Memphis and that one of the bridges across the curving river was bright with lights.

15

It was twilight on a clear, gold, late-summer day that almost had a hum to it, a chord in a minor key. Ed was in the backyard of the Half Moon Hotel. He had just finished watering some pitiful potted geraniums that someone had put back there and forgotten about, when he turned around and there was Jack Hawn standing in the middle of the yard. Ed hadn't seen Jack in several years, but there he stood with his hands in his jean pockets. In the twilight he didn't look all that real to Ed; his light shirt and light jeans made him seem to float above the yard. It was an illusion. This was Jack, his son-in-law, Janet's husband, a man the father of a daughter would naturally have mixed feelings about.

Ed pulled his shoes out of the mud below the spigot and motioned for Jack to have a seat. In that ridiculous little chair Jack seemed substantial enough, and heavy. Ed turned the water off, and drying his hands on his pants, sighing at his uneasiness and reluctance, went to sit beside Jack.

Jack didn't say anything, but leaned back in the chair, precarious on its two wobbly legs, his hands on his heavy thighs. He seemed to be holding his breath. He didn't speak. This was odd for Jack, who usually filled the air around you with his big voice and with gestures that you sometimes had to back away from. While Jack looked up at the locust tree, apparently thinking of what he would say, Ed realized that it was Jack's voice that gave Jack life. Before he spoke you would see him as a fattish middle-aged man with a coarsening, broad face and not much light in the eyes. You might not give him another look.

Ed waited for Jack to speak, but after a moment he spoke first. "Jack," he said, "when did you get in?"

"Yesterday afternoon," Jack said, gesturing to Janet's room above them. Jack was still reluctant to talk. He was thinking things over. Ed wondered if Edith knew Jack was here, if it was Edith's doing that had brought him here. He wondered why Janet hadn't called him. But most of all he wondered at himself: over the last month or over the summer he had somehow forgotten Jack, forgotten to hold him in his mind the way he had held him for years—almost as a son. He wondered if Janet still held him in her mind.

Finally, Jack sighed and set down the chair on all four legs. It was Jack Hawn who sat there, but it was also a stranger—much larger than Ed would have expected him to be, and there was something hard about his mouth that he would not have expected of Jack Hawn. But in the face whose edges had blurred was still that strong Hawn face—stubborn and boyish.

Then Ed saw that Jack had set aside whatever idea or errand had brought him here. He again leaned back in the chair, punching its legs deeper into the lawn and spoke, taking up the teasing tone he'd always used on Ed, or something close to it. "You look pretty good for such a busy old guy, Ed—bossing and running all these women. I let my concentration go a little and you take back your daughter—my wife—and put her up here in these luxurious accommodations." Like a big brush, his hand swiped at the peeling hotel behind him. "You get my brother to take you down to Tennessee or someplace to get a pacemaker put in, and you find that little kid, Vickie, and bring her up here and she brings a nice little package with her. You get your former wife to buy back the Check farm and offer me the lease." Jack put a heavy hand on Ed's shoulder and shook it. "You are a busy man. What else have you been up to?" Jack's smile was unreadable—warm and hostile—and that and all that energy and the sheer bulk of him caused the familiar speechless confusion in Ed that he'd noticed in Janet, too. It was part of the way Jack worked on the world. Ed just laughed and shook his head. "Are you taking the lease?" he asked.

Jack's smile faded. "That depends," he said. And he got up and walked toward the locust tree, stopping just short of its feathery reach. The tree was beginning to catch the lowering sun. "You know this guy Nelson Alvin?" Jack wasn't asking Ed; he was assuming this was the case.

"Yes?" Ed said.

"You probably know he's had this . . . thing with Janet. She told me about it. She says it's over and I believe her, I think. Hell, I'm not perfect, but what I want to know is who knows about this? Do you think I can come back here and live?" Jack was watching Ed's face closely.

Ed got up and walked across the grass to the spigot. He began coiling up the hose. After a minute Jack followed him and took the hose out of his hands. He coiled it neatly and quickly and then, with his hand on Ed's elbow, led Ed back to the chairs.

Ed sat down. Jack stood in front of him. "You didn't know?" Jack said.

"No, I didn't," Ed said. The lie surprised him, but it was the least he could do.

"I'm glad you didn't know." Ed didn't say anything,

and Jack continued. "Because if *you* didn't know, no one knew. And that answers my question."

"So you're going to stick around?"

"I want to," he said. "There are things I think I can do here, and it's good to be back. For the most part."

They talked some more, though Ed could see that Jack couldn't wait to get away. But first he had to bury that little bit of conversation under more talk.

They talked about Janet's new job at the nursing home, how she seemed to like it. "Yeah," said Jack, "she's always liked older people."

"I know," Ed said. "She's nuts about me."

They laughed about Carl and Ed bringing Vickie here to the hotel, and how that did not set right with Edith. And Vickie didn't like it either. "She actually stamped her foot one day at something Edith said about a home for unwed mothers." Ed and Jack both laughed, enjoying the picture of her little foot and her big temper. "And the funny thing is, Jackie, that Edith liked it too. I think Edith, against her better judgment, is starting to take to Vickie."

Now Jack seemed relaxed and lively, more like the old Jack. The edge of hostility had disappeared. "I'm glad you're back, bud," Ed told him. "I hope you stay. I hope you do take the lease."

Jack stood up. "The thing is, Ed, I don't know if I want to farm now. I don't know if it makes sense these days. I don't know if it makes sense for a middle-aged fat guy like me to take on all those acres and debts and drive up and down a field on a tractor thinking my nasty thoughts and go home to live in a house with my brother. I'm too old for all that."

"What do you want to do?"

Jack looked hard at Ed for a minute before he spoke, trying to decide if he could say whatever outrageous thing was in his mind. He stepped back and looked up at the Half Moon Hotel behind Ed. "I want to paint this place," he said. And he grinned and waved and then he was gone.

When Jack left, Ed sat there awhile and watched the sun leave the yard; it lit only the big locust tree, filling it with light as if it were a balloon filling with glowing gases.

The locust tree and all its ferny branches seemed to be slowly rising away from him; the grass cooled, and cold earth vapors rose beneath his chair. Ed shivered.

There was this . . . distance. He shivered again. They all seemed so far away, yet he could see them so clearly. He could see that Jack would paint the place; he would be the one, finally, to finish the eight-year renovation of the lobby, scrape and paint, and cut down the shrubs that blocked the light. Jack would be the one who could stand up to Edith and jolly her along and keep a crew of painters on the job. And he and Janet could live together, if Jack got a chance to do good work. Jack and Janet would talk Edith into letting Carl take the lease, have another chance at the farm now that he'd quit drinking. Vickie would insist on a place for herself and her baby. Mary would go on living alone in her little house and probably never know that her former husband's natural son beat up his mother, Deb Whiteside, now and then. He saw them all, but they were far away.

And Nelson had drifted away — partly because he was seeing Deb Whiteside, partly because he seemed to be working his way through more prominent citizens of Half Moon than Ed Check, but mostly because Ed had nothing to say to him anymore.

Edith, too, seemed distant, not blocking his way anymore. Lately, as far as he could tell, Ed didn't even exist for Edith; she didn't even stoop to ignore him. Ed wondered if all this mattered to him. He wondered if he cared.

Very close, in the nearest branch of the locust tree there was a little yellow-green bird. Ed watched it—so neat inside its outline and so perfect in its details. He watched it appearing and disappearing, silently hopping from twig to tiny twig, searching and finding something he couldn't see—bugs, he figured. Then he *wanted* that bird. He wanted it brought close. He could feel it already in his hand—some kind of vireo probably—the smooth feather surface, the wing edge like the deckled edge of paper, its heat and pulse and dust, its twiggy reptile legs pushing in his palm. And he could look into that bright, warning, side-seeing eye. "I only set out one day to *talk* to Marlene," Ed said to the bird.

The bird flew away. "Right," he said to the bird. "What kind of a fool confuses curiosity and desire, and then thinks desire and love are the same thing?" Ed went into the hotel.

MARTHA BERGLAND's first novel *A Farm under a Lake* was published by Graywolf and Vintage in the United States, and in Great Britain, Sweden, and Germany. "An Embarrassment of Ordinary Riches," a short story first published in the *New England Review*, was reprinted in the *Pushcart XII* anthology and in *Love Stories for the Rest of Us*. Bergland teaches English at Milwaukee Area Technical College.

This book was designed by Will Powers. It is set in Century Oldstyle type by Stanton Publication Services, Inc., and manufactured by Quebecor-Fairfield on acid-free paper.